A CASE FOR PAUL TEMPLE

Francis Durbridge

WILLIAMS & WHITING

Cover design by Timo Schroeder

9781912582693

Williams & Whiting (Publishers)
15 Chestnut Grove, Hurstpierpoint,
West Sussex, BN6 9SS

Titles by Francis Durbridge published by Williams & Whiting

1   The Scarf – tv serial
2   Paul Temple and the Curzon Case – radio serial
3   La Boutique – radio serial
4   The Broken Horseshoe – tv serial
5   Three Plays for Radio Volume 1
6   Send for Paul Temple – radio serial
7   A Time of Day – tv serial
8   Death Comes to The Hibiscus – stage play
    The Essential Heart – radio play
    (writing as Nicholas Vane)
9   Send for Paul Temple – stage play
10 The Teckman Biography (tv serial)
11 Paul Temple and Steve (radio serial)
12 Twenty Minutes From Rome
13 Portrait of Alison
14 Paul Temple: Two Plays for Radio Volume 1
15 Three Plays for Radio Volume 2
16 The Other Man
17 Paul Temple and the Spencer Affair
18 Step In The Dark
19 My Friend Charles

Murder At The Weekend – the rediscovered newspaper serials
and short stories

Also published by Williams & Whiting:
Francis Durbridge : The Complete Guide
By Melvyn Barnes

INTRODUCTION

Francis Durbridge (1912-98) began his career in 1933 as a writer of sketches, stories and plays for BBC radio. They were mostly light entertainments, but a talent for crime fiction became evident in his radio plays *Murder in the Midlands* (1934) and *Murder in the Embassy* (1937).

He continued to write radio plays and serials for many years, using his own name and the pseudonyms Frank Cromwell, Nicholas Vane and Lewis Middleton Harvey, but his triumph was the creation of novelist/detective Paul Temple and his wife Steve. When the serial *Send for Paul Temple* was broadcast in 1938, listeners bombarded the BBC with over 7,000 requests for more and Durbridge responded later the same year with *Paul Temple and the Front Page Men*. Then from 1939 to 1968 there were another twenty-six Paul Temple radio productions, of which seven were new versions of earlier cases. In the mid-twentieth century radio detectives were extremely popular, with Paul Temple's rivals including Dick Barton (by Edward J. Mason), Philip Odell (by Lester Powell), Dr. Morelle (by Ernest Dudley), P.C. 49 (by Alan Stranks) and Ambrose West (by Philip Levene).

But Durbridge was to prove his versatility as a playwright and in 1952, while continuing to write for radio, he embarked on a sequence of BBC television serials (not featuring the Temples) that achieved huge viewing figures until 1980. And additionally, from 1971 in the UK and even earlier in Germany, he became known for stage plays that are still produced by professional and amateur companies today.

A Case for Paul Temple was broadcast in eight thirty-minute episodes, from 7 February to 28 March 1946. It was the sixth outing for Temple and Steve, and the only appearance by Howard Marion-Crawford (1914-69) as Temple. His successor was Kim Peacock (1901-66), who appeared nine times in the role from *Paul Temple and the Gregory Affair* (1946) until the 1953 one-hour play *Paul Temple and Steve Again*. Peacock was then replaced by the actor who became the definitive Paul Temple – Peter Coke (1913-2008), the much-remembered voice of *Paul Temple and the Gilbert Case* (1954) and every other serial until the concluding *Paul Temple and the Alex Affair* in 1968.

Leaving Temple himself aside, it would be criminal to forget the dulcet tones of Marjorie Westbury (1905-89), who appeared on BBC radio as an actress and singer in numerous Durbridge plays from the early 1930s and in *Paul Temple Intervenes* (the small part of Dolly Fraser) in 1942. She then made the role of Steve her own in *Send for Paul Temple Again* in 1945 for the first of twenty-three occasions until the final serial *Paul Temple and the Alex Affair* (1968). In the process she partnered both Peacock and Coke in all their appearances, and before Peacock she had played Steve opposite Barry Morse in *Send for Paul Temple Again* (1945) as well as Howard Marion-Crawford in *A Case for Paul Temple*. Nevertheless, Paul and Steve notwithstanding, mention must be made of Sir Graham Forbes of Scotland Yard, the role in which Lester Mudditt appeared on nineteen occasions from the original serial in 1938 until *Paul Temple and the Spencer Affair* in 1958.

The exploits of Paul Temple built an impressive UK and European fanbase, with the radio serials resulting in four cinema movies and numerous novels and the Paul Temple brand spawning a syndicated newspaper strip from December 1950 to May 1971 and a television series from 1969 to 1971 (though this was not written by Durbridge). And on the Continent, Paul Temple radio serials were broadcast in translation and using their own actors from 1939 in the Netherlands, from 1949 in Germany, from 1953 in Italy and from 1954 in Denmark.

European radio productions of *A Case for Paul Temple* began with the Dutch radio version *Paul Vlaanderen grijpt in* (6 October – 24 November 1946, eight episodes), translated by J.C. van der Horst and produced by Kommer Kleijn, with Jan van Ees as Vlaanderen and Eva Janssen as Ina. A few years later this was followed by the German radio version, *Ein Fall für Paul Temple* (10 February – 7 April 1951, eight episodes), translated by Marianne de Barde and produced by Eduard Hermann, with René Deltgen as Temple and Elisabeth Scherer as Steve; and the Italian radio version, *Paul Temple, il romanziere poliziotto* (28 January – 18 March 1953, eight episodes), produced by Umberto Benedetto, with Fernando Farese as Temple and Franca Mazzoni as Betty (not Steve). But this serial was revived yet again with a new German translation by Georg Pagitz, *Paul Temple und der Fall Valentine*, for streaming and on CDs from 22 April 2022 but not yet broadcast on radio, produced by Antonio F. Lopez, with Matthias Kiel as Temple and Katja Keßler as Steve. And in advance of this there was an abridged online broadcast called *Ein Fall für Paul Temple*, adapted and produced by Klaus Krückemeyer (who also played Temple) on 12 June 2021.

In the UK in 2006 the BBC provided clear evidence that Durbridge's name was not forgotten, when it gave an enormous fillip to Paul Temple fans by taking surviving radio scripts and re-creating the broadcasts with present-day actors and traditional sound effects. The first of these, *Paul Temple and the Sullivan Mystery* (from 1948), was followed by *Paul Temple and the Madison Mystery* (from 1949), *Paul Temple and Steve* (from 1947), *A Case for Paul Temple* (from 1946) and *Paul Temple and the Gregory Affair* (from 1946) – all produced by Patrick Rayner, and breathing new life into these serials for many listeners who could not have heard the originals. And in respect of *A Case for Paul Temple*, this was broadcast from 24 August to 12 October 2011 and marketed on

CDs (AudioGO, 2011), also included in the CD set *Paul Temple: The Complete Radio Collection: Paul Temple Returns* 2006-2013, BBC, 2017.

Melvyn Barnes
Author of *Francis Durbridge: The Complete Guide* (Williams & Whiting, 2018)

This book reproduces Francis Durbridge's original script together with the list of characters and actors of the BBC programme on the dates mentioned, but the eventual broadcast might have edited Durbridge's script in respect of scenes, dialogue and character names.

A CASE FOR PAUL TEMPLE

A serial in eight episodes

By FRANCIS DURBRIDGE

Broadcast on BBC Radio

7 February – 28 March 1946

CAST:

Paul Temple . .Howard Marion-Crawford
Steve, his wife . . . . . Marjorie Westbury
Sir Graham Forbes . . . . . .Lester Mudditt
Major Peters . . . . Cyril Gardiner
Charles Kelvin . . . . Olaf Olsen
Superintendent Wetherby . .Gilbert Davis
                              and Laidman Browne
Sheila Baxter . . . . .Rita Vale
Gillespie . . . . .Duncan McIntyre
Snooker Riley . . . . Frank Partington
Joy . . . . Lucille Lisle
Captain O'Hara . . . . .Tommy Duggan
Sir Gilbert Dryden . . . . Alexander Sarner
Mary . . . . Dorothy Smith
Daisy . . . . .Vivienne Chatterton
Mr Layland . . . . .Tommy Duggan
Commentator . . . . .Denis Webb
Jules Condré . . . . Leslie Perrins
Sergeant Hodson . . . . Frank Atkinson
Other parts played by Beryl Calder,
Charles Leno and members of the
BBC Drama Repertory Company

A CASE FOR PAUL TEMPLE

A NEW PRODUCTION

Broadcast on BBC Radio
24 August – 12 October 2011
CAST:

Paul Temple . . . . Crawford Logan
Steve, his wife . . . . Gerda Stevenson
Sir Graham Forbes . . . . . Gareth Thomas
Major Peters . . . . .Greg Powrie
Charles Kelvin . . . . Nick Underwood
Superintendent Wetherby

Richard Greenwood

Sheila Baxter . . . . Melody Grove
Snooker Riley . . . . .Jimmy Chisholm
Joy . . . . .Lucy Paterson
Captain O'Hara . . . . .Robin Laing
Sir Gilbert Dryden . . Michael Mackenzie
Mary . . . . .Eliza Langland
Mr Layland . . . . .Robin Laing
Jules Condré . . . . John Paul Hurley
Superintendent Bradley . . . . . Simon Tait
Other parts played by members of the cast

EPISODE ONE

IN WHICH PAUL TEMPLE HEARS ABOUT VALENTINE

OPEN TO:

The sound of a crowded thoroughfare. An extremely large and excited crowd of people are watching one of the buildings near Oxford Circus.

Quickly FADE away from each voice: as if we are moving across the voice of the crowd.

GIRL: (*Staggered*) You mean to say she's going to commit suicide!

2ND GIRL: My Gawd, you wouldn't get me jumping off a roof, not for all the gin in London!

MAN: How did she get up there in the first place, that's what I'd like to know!

WOMAN: If she's goin' to jump, I wish to Gawd she'd jump!

2ND MAN: She's only a youngster by the look of things – can't be more than twenty-two or three!

2ND WOMAN: The number of people what seem to be doin' themselves in, why I've never 'eard of so many suicides in one week …

3RD MAN: (*Educated voice: rather indignantly*) I say. Can't someone get onto the roof? I mean, surely, there must be an entrance of some sort or …

4TH MAN: I don't think so, old boy, they've been trying to do that for the last (*Suddenly: a quick gasp from the crowd*) … Hello! She's moving!

5TH MAN: If you want my opinion, she's funking it! You can see what's happened, the stupid girl …

Quick FADE UP of a passing ambulance.

FADE AWAY ambulance and FADE UP of TONY banging a telephone receiver. TONY is in a telephone booth: background of the crowded thoroughfare.

3

TONY: (*On the phone*) Hello! Hello! Hello!

GIRL: (*On the other end*) Daily Tribune …

TONY: (*Quickly, irritated*) This is Hanson – give me Frank
          Rogers …

ROGERS: (*After a moment: coming through*) Hello? Who's
          that?

TONY: Frank? This is Tony …

ROGERS: (*Tensely*) What the heck's happening? I thought
          you'd gone on your holidays!

TONY: (*Quietly*) Frank, stop acting like a Hollywood editor
          and listen to what I'm saying. I don't think this kid's
          going to commit suicide after all.

ROGERS: What d'you mean?!!! Not going to commit
          suicide!!!   She's got to commit suicide! We've
          got the whole story written up – the moment she
          jumps we go to press. Tony, don't you realise
          there's been nine suicides this week! Nine suicides!
          If this girl jumps …

TONY: (*Quickly*) Just a minute! (*Peering*) She's climbing
          out onto a ledge over on the east side of the
          building, it … looks … to … me … as … if …
          (*Hesitates*)

ROGERS: (*Tensely: impatiently*) What is it? What's
          happening?

TONY: (*Moved*) This … is … awful ... she's …

ROGERS: What is it?!!! What is it?!!! What's happening?!!!
          Tony for heaven's …

There is a sudden scream: a wild surge forward of the crowd.
A significant silence falls on the crowd.

TONY: (*Quietly*) O.K. Frank, you can print it!
Quick FADE UP of MUSIC.

*FADE DOWN of MUSIC and FADE UP of a car which
gradually slows down and comes to a standstill. The car door*

4

opens and closes. Footsteps can be heard. The sound of a bell pull and then the distant clanging of an old-fashioned bell. After a moment, WETHERBY speaks. SUPERINTENDENT WETHERBY is a man of about fifty. He has a brisk manner and a slight north county accent.

WETHERBY: M'm - I can never understand why these places are so out of the way. (*A moment*) Ever been to one before?

KELVIN: (*Nervously, halting*) No … No, I'm afraid I haven't. *CHARLES KELVIN is an Austrian; about twenty-eight.*

WETHERBY: Always got such a confounded air of mystery about 'em! Don't know why, I'm sure! Just look at this place …

KELVIN: (*Quietly*) You know what Shakespeare said about death …

WETHERBY: Shakespeare? Not much in my line I'm afraid … (*Suddenly*) Ah, here we are!

The door is opened.

WETHERBY: Mr Gillespie?

GILLESPIE: (*A dour, wizened little Scotsman: he is not sinister*) Aye …

WETHERBY: (*With authority*) My name is Wetherby. Superintendent Wetherby of the Criminal Investigation Department, New Scotland …

GILLESPIE: (*Interrupting WETHERBY: not impressed*) I know … I know … I've been expecting ye. Will ye come in please?

WETHERBY: Thank you.

The door closes.

WETHERBY: Oh, er – this is Mr Kelvin …

GILLESPIE: Mr …?

KELVIN: (*Nervously*) Kelvin. Charles Kelvin …

5

GILLESPIE: (*Peering at KELVIN*) Is this the first time ye've been to a mortuary, Mr Kelvin?

KELVIN: (*Hesitant*) Yes, I … er … the first time.

GILLESPIE: Well, I hope you'll be able to identify the poor wee thing. 'Tis the lassie ye be wanting to see, the one that committed suicide?

WETHERBY: Yes …

GILLESPIE: Well, over … here … gentlemen …

GILLESPIE draws a curtain aside.

Pause.

WETHERBY: (*With authority*) Well, Mr Kelvin? Do you recognise her?

KELVIN: (*Quietly: dully*) Yes, I recognise her, Superintendent. (*A pause*) … She's my wife …

Quick FADE UP of MUSIC.

Slow FADE DOWN of MUSIC.

FADE UP of a flat buzzer.

The buzzer continues and then we hear PAUL TEMPLE approaching. TEMPLE is humming to himself. He sounds gay and very pleased with life. He opens the door.

TEMPLE: (*Astonished*) By Timothy! By Timothy, if it isn't Scotland Yard!

FORBES: (*Laughing*) Hello, Temple! How are you?

TEMPLE: I'm fine, but I didn't expect to see you at … (*Suddenly*) Come in! Come in, Sir Graham! Come in!

FORBES: This is a colleague of mine … Major Peters … Paul Temple …

TEMPLE: Come in, Major!

The door closes.

PETERS: (*A pleasant, well-spoken man of about forty-five*) I'm awfully glad to meet you, Mr Temple,

6

	I've heard quite a lot about you from Sir Graham.

TEMPLE: Sir Graham and I are old friends we …

STEVE: (*Interrupting PAUL: calling from the bedroom*) Who is it, darling?

TEMPLE: (*Confidentially to PETERS*) That's my wife! She's dressing for dinner – she's been dressing since five o'clock! (*Raising his voice*) I'll give you three guesses!

FORBES: (*Calling*) Hello, Steve!

STEVE: (*From the bedroom*) Sir Graham! (*Lightly, but quickly*) Darling, whatever he says the answer's "No!"

TEMPLE: (*Laughing*) You're telling me! (*Brightly*) Come along, Sir Graham … Major Peters … let's go into the lounge …

FORBES: (*Start FADE*) You look very fit, Temple, although perhaps a little tired about the eyes …

Complete FADE.

FADE UP the sound of glasses clinking …

TEMPLE: Well – your very good health, Sir Graham!

FORBES: Thank you, Temple!

PETERS: Skoal!

TEMPLE: Skoal!

FORBES: And how's the son and heir?

TEMPLE: Oh, he's fine. He's down at Bramley Lodge at the moment with Nannie. Steve and I are staying in Town for three or four days.

FORBES: You're dining out tonight, I take it?

TEMPLE: Yes, as a matter of fact I was just going to get dressed. Oh, excuse the dressing gown. It's my wife's idea of what the popular novelist should wear.

7

PETERS laughs.

TEMPLE: Strictly between ourselves, I've never been to China.

SIR GRAHAM and PETERS laugh.

A tiny pause.

FORBES: I don't think you've met Major Peters before?

TEMPLE: (*Pleasantly*) No, I don't think I have, Sir Graham.

FORBES: Peters was attached to the Intelligence people during the war – he's just been transferred to our Special Branch at Scotland Yard.

TEMPLE: Oh, I see.

PETERS: (*With a little laugh*) Rather a square peg in a round hole I'm afraid, sir.

FORBES: You'll settle down.

A moment's pause.

TEMPLE: (*Suddenly: deliberately breaking the pause*) Would you like a cigar, Sir Graham, or …

FORBES: No, I'm – er – I don't think so … thanks.

A second pause.

PETERS: (*Seriously: quietly*) Don't you think it might be rather a good idea if we came straight to the point, sir?

TEMPLE: That's always a good idea, Major.

FORBES: (*With a very serious note in his voice*) Just after three thirty this afternoon, a girl committed suicide. Her name was Myra Kelvin. She threw herself off the roof of …

TEMPLE: (*Interrupting FORBES, apparently completely disinterested*) Yes, it's – in the papers …

FORBES: That suicide was the tenth! The tenth suicide to take place in London during the past week. (*A moment*) Doesn't that strike you as being particularly significant?

8

TEMPLE:	(*Politely*) Significant?
FORBES:	Yes.
TEMPLE:	(*Innocently*) I don't think so, Sir Graham …
PETERS:	(*Quietly, astounded*) Mr Temple, ten people have committed suicide in the West End of London within the space of seven days! And yet you don't think that …
TEMPLE:	(*Interrupting PETERS*) Major Peters, I am by profession a novelist. I write – for my sins – detective novels. At the present moment, I am engaged on a new opus significantly entitled "Over My Dead Body!" My contract stipulates eighty thousand words. I have written precisely two thousand three hundred and fifty-four. If I have no interruptions, if I am left entirely alone, if I work from nine in the morning until nine at night, there is a remote possibility that by the middle of next September I shall have completed …
PETERS:	(*Interrupting TEMPLE: annoyed*) In other words you're not interested!
TEMPLE:	(*Politely*) In other words – I'm not interested.
FORBES:	(*With obvious sincerity: perturbed*) Temple, listen! When I've come to you for help in the past, I've done so because – I felt convinced that things were so desperate that we needed not merely a new perspective, but …
TEMPLE:	(*Quietly, seriously*) What's on your mind, Sir Graham?

A moment.

FORBES:	For the past three months, Major Peters, Superintendent Wetherby and myself, have been investigating a case known to us at Scotland Yard as The Granger Affair. Three

9

months ago, a girl called Lesley Granger committed suicide. There was an inquest, and it was discovered that Lesley Granger had been taking drugs – cocaine. She had been getting the cocaine presumably from a secret source. From a man – or woman – known to her quite simply as – Valentine.

TEMPLE: Valentine?

FORBES: Two days after Lesley Granger committed suicide, a girl called Marjorie Barton died under mysterious circumstances. Once again there was an inquest – and an autopsy.

TEMPLE: (*Interested*) She'd been taking drugs?

FORBES: Yes.

TEMPLE: Cocaine?

FORBES: No. No, in this particular instance – heroin.

TEMPLE: Go on …

FORBES: Every person that's committed suicide during the past three months has – without exception – been a drug addict.

TEMPLE: Are you suggesting that …

FORBES: I'm suggesting that there exists in the West End of London, at the present moment, a secret organisation trafficking exclusively in dangerous drugs. That organisation is growing, Temple. It's growing so rapidly that unless we can put our fingers on the person who controls it – unless we can find the …

PETERS: (*Ominously*) Unless we can find this mysterious Mr Valentine, there's going to be a new crime wave in this country: a crime wave quite without precedent.

FORBES: Believe me, that's no exaggeration!

A pause.

TEMPLE:	Sir Graham, tell me: are you convinced – quite convinced – that the people who committed suicide were in contact – in direct contact – with Valentine?
FORBES:	Yes. Yes, we're quite convinced of that, Temple.
PETERS:	And there's another point, Mr Temple, er – just in case you're interested. We found a compact on Marjorie Barton – a powder compact. Scribbled on the back of the compact was apparently a person's name. The name was Simon Lee.
TEMPLE:	Simon Lee?
FORBES:	Yes. Go on, Peters.
PETERS:	Early this evening, Superintendent Wetherby interviewed a young man called Charles Kelvin …
FORBES:	… He's the husband of the girl that committed suicide this afternoon – as a matter of fact he identified the body.
TEMPLE:	Yes …
PETERS:	During the course of cross examination, Kelvin admitted that his wife had been – difficult – highly strung – emotional. On two occasions – during a hysterical outburst – he remembers quite distinctly that she repeated the name Simon Lee.
TEMPLE:	Did the name have any particular significance, so far as Kelvin himself was concerned?
PETERS:	No. He's just as puzzled as we are. He's never even heard of anyone called Simon Lee.
TEMPLE:	M'm. (*Dismissing the matter*) Well, you seem to have an interesting case on your hands, Sir Graham. I only wish I had time to …

FORBES: (*Interrupting: perturbed*) Temple! This business can't be treated lightly. If this organisation develops …

TEMPLE: (*Appalled*) But it mustn't be allowed to develop, Sir Graham!

FORBES: (*Ominously*) I'm afraid our methods – orthodox methods – are not always the best in a case of this kind.

TEMPLE: You mean …?

FORBES: I mean – to put it frankly – that, in my opinion, this is … A Case for Paul Temple.

A moment.

TEMPLE: Well – what do you want me to do exactly?

PETERS: Don't you know? (*A moment: quietly*) We want you to catch Valentine, Mr Temple.

A tiny pause, then TEMPLE suddenly laughs.

TEMPLE: (*Snapping his fingers*) Just like that!

PETERS: Well, after all, according to all accounts you caught The Knave – The Front Page Man – Z4 – The Marquis … and … even … Rex.

A moment.

FORBES: What do you say, Temple …?

TEMPLE: (*Seriously*) What can I say, Sir Graham?

FORBES: (*Eagerly*) You mean?

TEMPLE: I mean … (*Suddenly, changing his mind*) Let's all have another glass of sherry!

FADE UP of MUSIC.

FADE DOWN of MUSIC and CROSS FADE the sound of a small, rather pleasant, dance orchestra. They are playing a modern – but not too noisy – dance number.

FADE ACROSS to the Temple's table.

WAITER: Your change, sir.

TEMPLE: That's all right, waiter – keep the change.

12

WAITER: Thank you, sir. I hope everything has been satisfactory.

TEMPLE: Everything's been fine, Luigi – thank you.

WAITER: Thank you, sir.

The WAITER departs.

A moment.

TEMPLE: Shall I fetch the car?

STEVE: Where is it?

TEMPLE: It's in the mews just round the corner.

STEVE: No, it's all right, darling, I'll walk round with you.

TEMPLE: O.K.

STEVE: (*After a moment*) Paul …

TEMPLE: (*Casually: lighting a cigarette*) Yes, Steve?

STEVE: (*Quietly*) You still haven't told me …

TEMPLE: Told you what, darling?

STEVE: You still haven't told me what Sir Graham wanted.

TEMPLE: (*Faintly amused*) Don't you know what he wanted?

STEVE: What do you mean?

TEMPLE: Darling, I'm quite convinced that you had your ear glued to the lounge door from the moment Sir Graham arrived, so there's not the slightest necessity for me to tell you what …

STEVE: (*Highly indignant*) Why, you beast! What – what a horrible suggestion!

TEMPLE: Well – didn't you?

STEVE: Most certainly not! I – I …

TEMPLE: Didn't you?!

STEVE: Well, I … I may have overheard a little of the conversation of course, but … (*Suddenly*) Yes, I did listen! So there!

TEMPLE: (*Laughing at STEVE*) So there! (*Amused*) Steve, don't look so serious!

13

A moment.

STEVE: What are you going to do?

TEMPLE: (*Completely off-hand, almost gay*) What do you think I'm going to do? I'm going to finish the novel I'm writing – it doesn't matter two hoots to me if fifty people commit suicide. Let 'em all commit suicide if they want to – the more the merrier.

STEVE: But you heard what Sir Graham said …

TEMPLE: Of course I heard!

STEVE: (*Seriously*) If this organisation is allowed to develop …

TEMPLE: But it mustn't be allowed to develop! What's Sir Graham doing and all the bright little boys at Scotland Yard? Good gracious me, if they're going to send for Paul Temple at the least …

STEVE: Paul, you know as well as I do, that if Sir Graham didn't consider this matter of paramount importance, he would never have come.

TEMPLE: I say, look here, do you want me to get mixed up in this business?

STEVE: (*Quickly*) Oh, darling, of course I don't!

TEMPLE: Well, what's all the fuss about? I'm not going to get mixed up in it! Don't be so silly, darling! I can sit back with my feet on the mantlepiece the same as the next fellow!

STEVE: (*Almost convinced*) Of course if you feel like that, Paul …

TEMPLE: (*Carried away, overdoing it*) You bet your bottom dollar I feel like that! Yes, sir! We're a pretty staid married couple these days, Steve – and don't you forget it. Why, believe

14

me, Steve, the thoughts of getting mixed up in anything so exciting – so dangerous – as the Valentine affair positively appals me! Positively appals me, old girl! Why … (*Aside*) Oh, waiter, my bill …

STEVE: (*Suspicious of TEMPLE's act*) You've paid the bill.

TEMPLE: What? Oh, yes! Oh, yes, so I have. (*Forcefully*) Darling, do you know what I said to Sir Graham? Do you know what I said to Sir Graham when he had the audacity to suggest that this was a case for Paul Temple?

STEVE: No, what did you say?

TEMPLE: I said … Sir Graham, I said … I … I … (*Weakly, off his guard*) I'd like to think it over.

STEVE: (*Significantly*) Yes. Yes, that's what I thought you said! (*A moment, then STEVE starts to laugh*) Come along – let's get our things …

FADE UP of dance orchestra.

FADE DOWN to the background.

CLOAKROOM ATTENDANT: Had you an umbrella, sir?

TEMPLE: No, just the overcoat.

ATTENDANT: Thank you, sir.

TEMPLE: Thank you. (*Turning – pleasantly*) Oh, hello, Superintendent!

WETHERBY: (*Taken by surprise*) I beg your pardon, I … (*Suddenly*) Oh, good evening, Mr Temple! I'm afraid I didn't recognise you, sir.

TEMPLE: Are you just arriving or leaving?

WETHERBY: No. No, as a matter of fact, I'm just leaving. (*Pleasantly*) Ah, good evening, Mrs Temple!

TEMPLE: You remember Superintendent Wetherby?

15

STEVE: Yes, of course!

TEMPLE: Can we give you a lift, Wetherby, my car's just round the corner?

WETHERBY: No, I don't think so, thanks all the same, sir – but I'll stroll along to the corner with you.

TEMPLE, STEVE and WETHERBY are leaving the restaurant.

WETHERBY: I hear that Sir Graham and Major Peters paid you a visit this evening?

Start to FADE Scene.

TEMPLE: Yes. Yes, as a matter of fact they did …

WETHERBY: … I don't know whether they managed to interest you in this extraordinary affair.

FADE SCENE.

FADE UP of TEMPLE's voice and the sound of TEMPLE, STEVE and SUPERINTENDENT WETHERBY strolling along the pavement.

TEMPLE: … I'm afraid I told Sir Graham more or less what I'm telling you, Superintendent.

WETHERBY: M'm. Well, generally speaking, I don't welcome outsiders, you know that, Mr Temple. In fact, my opinion of amateur detectives is nobody's business!

TEMPLE laughs.

WETHERBY: But I must confess after the way you handled the Rex affair …

TEMPLE: I'd a certain amount of luck over the Rex affair.

WETHERBY: We all need a certain amount of luck, sir – that goes without saying.

STEVE: Where's the car, darling?

TEMPLE: M'm? Oh, it's just down here, Steve, in the mews. Stay with the Superintendent – I shan't be a minute.

TEMPLE departs.

WETHERBY: How long are you staying in Town, Mrs Temple?

STEVE: Oh, only for two or three days. (*Start to FADE voice*) I suppose I really ought to be down at Bramley Lodge, but I promised my husband that we'd spend a few days in ...

COMPLETE FADE.

FADE UP of TEMPLE approaching his car: he is whistling softly to himself. He reaches the car and throws open the door.

TEMPLE: (*Surprised, taken aback*) Why ...

JOY: (*A girl of about thirty: a strange note of desperation in her voice*) Mr Temple, don't move, I ...

TEMPLE: What are you doing? What are you doing hiding in my car? Who are you, and ...

JOY: (*Desperately*) Mr Temple, please listen to me! Listen to me! You've got to listen to me, Mr Temple, I ... (*She is apparently in pain*) I ... I ...

TEMPLE: What is it? Are you hurt?

JOY: (*Weakly*) Yes ... Yes ... It's my arm ... I ... (*Suddenly*) But listen! Listen! I – I want to tell you something ... I want to tell you something about ... about ... about Simon Lee ...

TEMPLE: (*Quietly, staggered*) Simon Lee! Why ...

JOY gives a sudden groan and faints.

TEMPLE: Oh, dash, she's fainted! (*Suddenly, shouting*) Wetherby! Wetherby!

TEMPLE slams the door of the car and starts to run.

FADE.

FADE UP of SUPERINTENDENT WETHERBY.

WETHERBY: … I quite see your point of view, Mrs Temple, on the other hand, if Scotland Yard feel justified in consulting your … (*He stops*)

TEMPLE: (*From the background*) Wetherby! (*He is drawing near*)

STEVE: (*Alarmed*) What is it?

WETHERBY: Why, it looks to me as if …

TEMPLE arrives.

TEMPLE: (*Breathlessly*) Didn't you hear me shouting?

STEVE: (*Alarmed*) What is it? What's the matter, darling?

TEMPLE: There's a girl in my car – I think she's been hurt and she …

WETHERBY: She what?

TEMPLE: (*Quietly*) I think she was hiding there …

WETHERBY: (*Puzzled*) Hiding? In your car?

TEMPLE: Yes.

WETHERBY: (*Sounding rather dubious*) Is she badly hurt?

TEMPLE: I don't know.

WETHERBY: Well – come along – let's have a look at her! (*Start FADE*) Where is the car?

TEMPLE: It's almost at the end of the mews …

COMPLETE FADE.

FADE UP of footsteps.

TEMPLE: Here we are!

TEMPLE opens the car door again.

A pause.

WETHERBY: Well – where is she?

STEVE: Darling, there's no one here!

TEMPLE: (*Astonished*) But – but she was here a moment ago!

STEVE: Well, there's no one here now, Paul!

WETHERBY: (*Suspiciously*) Is this some kind of a joke, Mr Temple, because …

TEMPLE: Of course it isn't a joke! She was here – lying on the front seat!

WETHERBY: Well, she's not here now!

TEMPLE: (*Faintly annoyed*) But the girl was in pain, she couldn't have moved without … (*Suddenly*) Look here! This is a cul-de-sac, she didn't pass us coming down to the car so she must still be here in the mews …

WETHERBY: But there's nowhere for her to hide! There isn't a doorway – a building – or anything – it's just a brick wall! (*Peering*) Unless she's standing in the shadow over there at the bottom … Wait here! (*He departs*)

STEVE: (*Anxiously, in a quick whisper*) Paul, you did see her, didn't you?

TEMPLE: (*Irritatedly*) Of course I saw her! She spoke to me! She said …

STEVE: She said … what … darling?

TEMPLE: (*Quietly, thoughtfully*) She said: "I want to tell you … about … Simon Lee …"

STEVE: Simon Lee?

TEMPLE: Yes …

STEVE: But that doesn't make sense!

TEMPLE: Sh! Here's Wetherby!

The SUPERINTENDENT returns.

WETHERBY: Well, there's no one there, Mr Temple!

TEMPLE: Are you sure?

WETHERBY: Positive! There just isn't anywhere for the girl to hide! Why, a mouse couldn't hide itself in this mews!

TEMPLE: (*Almost losing his temper*) Well, she's not in the car! She didn't pass us! She's not at the

19

	bottom of the mews! There's nowhere for her to hide, so …
WETHERBY:	So what!!!!
TEMPLE:	(*Suddenly, a complete change: amused*) So I'm rather afraid that she must … have … just … vanished … into … thin … air, Superintendent. (*He is highly amused*) Come along, Steve – jump in the car – we'll go back to the flat!

FADE UP of MUSIC.

FADE DOWN of MUSIC.

STEVE:	(*Rather irritated*) Paul, you really are exasperating. I just can't understand you.
TEMPLE:	(*Still amused*) Can't you, my sweet?
STEVE:	You've been grinning like a Cheshire cat ever since we left the Superintendent!
TEMPLE:	A Cheshire cat! I resent that! I most strongly resent it!
STEVE:	A most extraordinary thing happens right under your very nose! Something which completely bewilders you …
TEMPLE:	What d'you mean – completely bewilders me? Who said it completely bewildered me? You speak for yourself, Mrs Temple!
STEVE:	But it must have bewildered you! The girl disappeared! Literally disappeared from right …
TEMPLE:	Right under my very nose! Yes, darling – you said that before! (*Changing the subject*) Gosh, I'm hungry! I could eat the hind legs off a turkey. I say, is there any of that cold chicken left in the … (*He is interrupted by the telephone ringing*) It's all right – I'll take it.

TEMPLE lifts the receiver.

SHEILA:	(*Tensely, on the other end of the wire*) Hello!
TEMPLE:	Hello?
SHEILA:	Hello!
TEMPLE:	Hello? (*Pleasantly*) Now it's your turn …
SHEILA:	(*There is no mistaking the seriousness in her voice*) Who – who is that, please?

A moment.

TEMPLE:	(*Seriously*) This is Mayfair 7894 …
SHEILA:	I – I want to speak to Paul Temple …
TEMPLE:	This is Temple speaking …
SHEILA:	Mr Temple – my name is Baxter – Sheila Baxter. I don't suppose you've heard of me, Mr Temple, but please listen to what I'm saying. Please listen most carefully – it's very urgent.

A moment.

TEMPLE:	Well?
SHEILA:	(*Lowering her voice to a soft yet extremely tense whisper*) Don't use the light – don't use the light in the bedroom, Mr Temple.
TEMPLE:	(*Taken aback*) What's that? What did you say?
SHEILA:	(*The same tense, urgent whisper*) I said … Don't use the light – don't use the light in the bedroom, Mr Temple …
TEMPLE:	(*Puzzled*) What do you mean, don't use the … (*SHEILA has replaced the receiver*) I say … Hello! (*He knocks the receiver*) Hello! Hello!!! (*Replacing the receiver: thoughtfully*) Well, I'm damned!
STEVE:	(*Noting PAUL's expression*) What is it? What's the matter?
TEMPLE:	Well – I – I don't know what to make of that, I'm sure!
STEVE:	What happened?

TEMPLE: Well – a woman's voice said: "My name is Baxter, Sheila Baxter. I don't suppose you've heard of me, Mr Temple, but please listen to what I'm saying". And then she said …

STEVE: And then she said what, darling?

TEMPLE: And then she said … "Don't use the light – don't use the light in the bedroom, Mr Temple" …

STEVE: Which bedroom?

TEMPLE: Well, I suppose she means our bedroom.

STEVE: What an extraordinary thing to say!

TEMPLE: (*Thoughtfully*) Yes …

STEVE: (*Suddenly*) Darling, this girl on the telephone, you don't think it was the girl …

TEMPLE: (*Still thinking*) No, it wasn't the girl in the mews – I'm sure of that. (*After a moment*) Stay here, Steve – I'm just going to take a look in the bedroom.

STEVE: (*Quickly*) No! No, I'll come with you, darling!

A door opens.

A second door is slowly opened.

TEMPLE: Well, everything seems to be all right …

STEVE: I don't know. We can't see very well with the …

TEMPLE: (*Quickly*) No! No, don't touch the switch! (*A tiny pause*) Wait a minute! Stand over there near the bed!

STEVE: (*Tensely*) What are you going to do?

TEMPLE: Don't move now, Steve!

STEVE: (*Alarmed*) Paul, what are you going to do?

TEMPLE: It's all right – now just keep still. (*Searching his pockets*) I've got an India-rubber in my pocket. I'm going to knock the switch on with the end of the rubber. Now stand still!

TEMPLE knocks the switch on: there is a deafening report of a revolver shot and the sudden smashing of glass as the bullet hits the bathroom door.

STEVE: (*Aghast, almost a scream*) Paul! Paul! Paul, are you
          …

TEMPLE: (*Calmly*) It's all right, darling – it's all right. Take it
          easy! Take it easy! (*A moment*) By Timothy, that's
          ingenious if you like!

STEVE: What was it?

TEMPLE: A revolver was wired up to the electric current and
          as soon as I touched the switch the revolver … By
          Timothy, it's lucky for me that revolver was a bit
          cock-eyed!

STEVE: Where – where is the gun?

TEMPLE: It's over there, by the bed-lamp …

STEVE: (*Bewildered*) But Paul, that must have been fitted
          up after we left the flat tonight …

TEMPLE: After Sir Graham left with Major Peters – yes.

STEVE: (*Suddenly, nervously*) Darling, don't let's get
          mixed up in this business, whatever happens, don't
          let's get …

TEMPLE: (*Staggered, amused*) Don't let's get mixed up in it!
          By Timothy, we seem to be in it up to the neck so
          far as I can make out! (*Quietly, thoughtfully*) You
          know, Steve – somebody must have known that Sir
          Graham was coming here! That trick with the
          revolver was a warning, a warning …

STEVE: A warning not to interfere …

TEMPLE: Yes.

STEVE: (*Interested in spite of herself*) Paul, you don't think
          that that mysterious person – the person Sir
          Graham called Valentine – planted the girl in your
          car and then deliberately …

TEMPLE: (*Prompting STEVE*) And then deliberately …?

STEVE: (*A moment, confused, thoughtfully*) I don't know
          … (*Suddenly, after a moment*) Supposing …

TEMPLE: Yes?

23

STEVE:	Supposing you did decide to investigate this business, then …
TEMPLE:	Then what?
STEVE:	Well – what would be the first …
TEMPLE:	The first thing I should do? The first thing I should do, darling, is to have a nice little chat with our old friend Snooker Riley.
STEVE:	Snooker Riley?
TEMPLE:	Yes. What Snooker doesn't know about the dope racket is nobody's business.
STEVE:	Is that the man that was mixed up in the Norwich case? The funny little cockney with …
TEMPLE:	Yes. He lives by himself on a houseboat over on the other side of Silverdale.
STEVE:	(*Intrigued*) On a houseboat?
TEMPLE:	Yes. (*A moment: quietly*) Why? What are you thinking?
STEVE:	Oh, I was just thinking. (*A moment: almost wistfully*) I've never been on a houseboat …

FADE UP of MUSIC.

FADE DOWN of MUSIC.
FADE UP of river noises: and then SLOW FADE up of the noise of a motor launch which continues for a little while.

SERGEANT:	There we are, sir! That's Snooker Riley's old tub!
TEMPLE:	Do you think you can pull alongside, Sergeant?
SERGEANT:	Sure! (*Pleasantly*) Hold on, Mrs Temple!

The launch pulls alongside the houseboat.

TEMPLE:	I'm very much obliged to you, Sergeant, for taking this trouble.
SERGEANT:	Only too glad to be of service, sir. Shall I pick you up in five or ten minutes?

TEMPLE:	I wish you would, Sergeant!
SERGEANT:	It's a pleasure, sir! (*Shouting with authority*) Snooker! Snooker!!!!
SNOOKER:	(*From the houseboat*) What the devil is it?
SERGEANT:	Jump to it you son of a gun! You've got visitors!!!
SNOOKER:	(*Nearer: peering over the side*) Visitors? What the devil do I want with visitors at this time o' the blessed ... (*Astonished*) ... Cor' Lummee!!!!
TEMPLE:	(*Laughing*) Hello Snooker!
SNOOKER:	(*Staggered*) Coo! God bless my soul, if it ain't Paul Temple!
TEMPLE:	How's the world been treating you, Snooker? Still in the dope racket?
SNOOKER:	Mr Temple! Please! Not in front of the Sergeant!

STEVE laughs.

SNOOKER:	'Ello, who's the piece of homework?
TEMPLE:	The piece of homework – as you so delicately put it – Snooker – is my wife.
SNOOKER:	Oh. (*Surprised*) Oh!
TEMPLE:	I take it you're still a bachelor?
SNOOKER:	Well – temporarily, Mr Temple, as you might say. Temporarily! (*Quickly*) 'Ere, give us your hand, Mrs T. I'll give you a leg up to the Cabin. (*Sharply*) Keep 'er steady, Sarge! Keep 'er steady!

FADE DOWN of the river noises.
COMPLETE FADE.

Quick FADE UP of the following scene in the cabin.

SNOOKER:	... Yes, I've 'ad this ole tub for twelve year or more. Gets a bit monotonous at times o' course

	but it's a cheap way o' living an' – well – I never was a one for gadding about, was I, Mr T?
TEMPLE:	(*Slowly, watching SNOOKER*) No, Snooker, you were never a one for gadding about. (*A tiny pause*) Snooker, tell me …
SNOOKER:	Yes, Guv'?
TEMPLE:	Tell me, have you heard of a woman called Sheila Baxter?
SNOOKER:	(*He hasn't heard of her*) Sheila Baxter? No – not that I know of. Why?
TEMPLE:	I … wondered … that's all. (*After a moment*) I take it you've heard of … Valentine?
SNOOKER:	(*Nervously*) Valentine? Yes – yes, I've 'eard of Valentine, but …
TEMPLE:	But what?
SNOOKER:	(*Quickly, tensely, rattled*) I don't know anything about 'im. Nothin' at all, see! I don't know whether Valentine's a man or a woman, I … I … I don't even know whether … (*Suddenly: suspicious*) Look 'ere, what's the game? You're the second bloke what's asked me about Valentine tonight – the second bloke what's …
TEMPLE:	(*Intrigued, interrupting SNOOKER*) Oh? Who was the first?
SNOOKER:	(*After a moment's hesitation*) A chap called Kelvin – Charles Kelvin.
TEMPLE:	Kelvin?
SNOOKER:	Yes, do you know 'im? Foreign sort o' bloke. Sounded to me a bit like a Jerry.
TEMPLE:	(*Slowly*) When did you see Mr Kelvin?

SNOOKER: About an hour ago. He came 'ere on his own. Borrowed a boat from a chap over at Silverdale.

TEMPLE: And he asked you about … Valentine?

SNOOKER: (*Quickly, unable to conceal a note of desperation*) Yes. Yes, 'e did. An' I told 'im what I'm telling you! I know nothin' about Valentine! Nothin'!!!

TEMPLE: (*Quietly, calming him*) All right, Snooker! All right!

A slight pause.

SNOOKER: (*With an effort*) Mr Temple, I've been a lot of things in my time, an' one way an' another, I've rubbed shoulders with a pretty mixed crowd of customers, but …

TEMPLE: But what, Snooker?

SNOOKER: But I've always 'ad a liking for you, Guv'nor, and so far as you're concerned, I've always – I've always tried to play the game.

TEMPLE: (*Slowly, watching SNOOKER*) Yes. Yes, I believe you have …

SNOOKER: Well – (*A pause, then*) Keep your nose out of this Valentine business, Mr Temple!!!! Take my advice an' keep your nose out of it!!!!

A pause.

TEMPLE: (*Quietly, as if he has been thinking about the matter*) Snooker, tell me, did you offer Mr Kelvin a drink?

SNOOKER: (*Surprised*) A drink? Why, no!

TEMPLE: (*Nodding*) I – I noticed the two glasses, on the side over there …

SNOOKER: (*Laughing*) Oh. Oh, that was O'Hara – a pal o'mine. Dropped in about six o'clock tonight. Regular old sea dog!

27

TEMPLE:	O'Hara?
SNOOKER:	Yes. Maybe you know him?
TEMPLE:	No. No, I can't say I do.
SNOOKER:	He's a card! You'd like O'Hara. (*Laughing*) Captain Michael Shaun Dougherty O'Hara … Skipper of The Simon Lee …
TEMPLE:	(*After a moment, dumbfounded*) The … Simon … Lee …?

FADE UP of MUSIC.

END OF EPISODE ONE

EPISODE TWO

IN WHICH STEVE
MEETS CAPTAIN O'HARA

OPEN TO:

ANNOUNCER: Paul Temple, the celebrated novelist and private detective, is visited by an old friend, Sir Graham Forbes, the Chief Commissioner of Scotland Yard, and by a Major Peters who is attached to the Special Branch of the Criminal Investigation Department. The following is a resumé of Episode One.

FADE UP SIR GRAHAM FORBES.

FORBES: For the past three months, Major Peters, Superintendent Wetherby and myself, have been investigating a case known to us at Scotland Yard as The Granger Affair. Three months ago, a girl called Lesley Granger committed suicide. There was an inquest, and it was discovered that Lesley Granger had been taking drugs – cocaine. She had been getting the cocaine presumably from a secret source. From a man – or woman – known to her quite simply as – Valentine.

TEMPLE: Valentine?

FORBES: Two days after Lesley Granger committed suicide, a girl called Marjorie Barton died under mysterious circumstances. Once again there was an inquest – and an autopsy.

TEMPLE: (*Interested*) She'd been taking drugs?

FORBES: Yes.

TEMPLE: Cocaine?

FORBES: No. No, in this particular instance – heroin.

TEMPLE: Go on ...

FORBES: Every person that's committed suicide during the past three months has – without exception – been a drug addict.

31

TEMPLE: Are you suggesting that …

FORBES: I'm suggesting that there exists in the West End of London, at the present moment, a secret organisation trafficking exclusively in dangerous drugs. That organisation is growing, Temple. It's growing so rapidly that unless we can put our fingers on the person who controls it – unless we can find the …

PETERS: (*Ominously*) Unless we can find this mysterious Mr Valentine, there's going to be a new crime wave in this country: a crime wave quite without precedent.

FORBES: Believe me, that's no exaggeration!

A pause.

TEMPLE: Sir Graham, tell me: are you convinced – quite convinced – that the people who committed suicide were in contact – in direct contact – with Valentine?

FORBES: Yes. Yes, we're quite convinced of that, Temple.

PETERS: And there's another point, Mr Temple, er – just in case you're interested. We found a compact on Marjorie Barton – a powder compact. Scribbled on the back of the compact was apparently a person's name. The name was Simon Lee.

TEMPLE: Simon Lee?

FORBES: Yes. Go on, Peters.

PETERS: Early this evening, Superintendent Wetherby interviewed a young man called Charles Kelvin …

FORBES: … He's the husband of the girl that committed suicide this afternoon – as a matter of fact he identified the body.

TEMPLE: Yes …

PETERS: During the course of cross examination, Kelvin admitted that his wife had been – difficult – highly strung – emotional. On two occasions – during a hysterical outburst – he remembers quite distinctly that she repeated the name Simon Lee.

TEMPLE: Did the name have any particular significance, so far as Kelvin himself was concerned?

PETERS: No. He's just as puzzled as we are. He's never even heard of anyone called Simon Lee.

TEMPLE: M'm. (*Dismissing the matter*) Well, you seem to have an interesting case on your hands, Sir Graham. I only wish I had time to …

FORBES: (*Interrupting: perturbed*) Temple! This business can't be treated lightly. If this organisation develops …

TEMPLE: (*Appalled*) But it mustn't be allowed to develop, Sir Graham!

FORBES: (*Ominously*) I'm afraid our methods – orthodox methods – are not always the best in a case of this kind.

TEMPLE: You mean …?

FORBES: I mean – to put it frankly – that, in my opinion, this is … A Case for Paul Temple.

A moment.

TEMPLE: Well – what do you want me to do exactly?

PETERS: Don't you know? (*A moment: quietly*) We want you to catch Valentine, Mr Temple.

A moment, then TEMPLE starts to laugh.

FADE laugh out.

ANNOUNCER: During the course of the same evening, Temple received a telephone message from a mysterious girl who introduced herself as Sheila Baxter. Later, Paul Temple, together with Steve his wife, visit Snooker Riley. Snooker is an old acquaintance of Temple's, and he lives, by himself, on a houseboat. He is a strange, rather disreputable little cockney.

FADE IN of SNOOKER.

SNOOKER: ... Yes, I've 'ad this ole tub for twelve year or more. Gets a bit monotonous at times o' course but it's a cheap way o' living an' – well – I never was a one for gadding about, was I, Mr T?

TEMPLE: (*Slowly, watching SNOOKER*) No, Snooker, you were never a one for gadding about. (*A tiny pause*) Snooker, tell me ...

SNOOKER: Yes, Guv'?

TEMPLE: Tell me, have you heard of a woman called Sheila Baxter?

SNOOKER: (*He hasn't heard of her*) Sheila Baxter? No – not that I know of. Why?

TEMPLE: I ... wondered ... that's all. (*After a moment*) I take it you've heard of ... Valentine?

SNOOKER: (*Nervously*) Valentine? Yes – yes, I've 'eard of Valentine, but ...

TEMPLE: But what?

SNOOKER: (*Quickly, tensely, rattled*) I don't know anything about 'im. Nothin' at all, see! I don't know whether Valentine's a man or a woman, I ... I ... I don't even know whether ... (*Suddenly: suspicious*) Look 'ere, what's the game? You're the second bloke what's asked me about Valentine tonight – the second bloke what's ...

TEMPLE: (*Intrigued, interrupting SNOOKER*) Oh? Who was the first?

SNOOKER: (*After a moment's hesitation*) A chap called Kelvin – Charles Kelvin.

34

TEMPLE: Kelvin?

SNOOKER: Yes, do you know 'im? Foreign sort o' bloke. Sounded to me a bit like a Jerry.

TEMPLE: (*Slowly*) When did you see Mr Kelvin?

SNOOKER: About an hour ago. He came 'ere on his own. Borrowed a boat from a chap over at Silverdale.

TEMPLE: And he asked you about … Valentine?

SNOOKER: (*Quickly, unable to conceal a note of desperation*) Yes. Yes, 'e did. An' I told 'im what I'm telling you! I know nothin' about Valentine! Nothin'!!!

TEMPLE: (*Quietly, calming him*) All right, Snooker! All right!

A slight pause.

SNOOKER: (*With an effort*) Mr Temple, I've been a lot of things in my time, an' one way an' another, I've rubbed shoulders with a pretty mixed crowd of customers, but …

TEMPLE: But what, Snooker?

SNOOKER: But I've always 'ad a liking for you, Guv'nor, and so far as you're concerned, I've always – I've always tried to play the game.

TEMPLE: (*Slowly, watching SNOOKER*) Yes. Yes, I believe you have …

SNOOKER: Well – (*A pause, then*) Keep your nose out of this Valentine business, Mr Temple!!!! Take my advice an' keep your nose out of it!!!!

A pause.

TEMPLE: (*Quietly, as if he has been thinking about the matter*) Snooker, tell me, did you offer Mr Kelvin a drink?

SNOOKER: (*Surprised*) A drink? Why, no!

TEMPLE: (*Nodding*) I – I noticed the two glasses, on the side over there …

SNOOKER: (*Laughing*) Oh. Oh, that was O'Hara – a pal o' mine. Dropped in about six o'clock tonight. Regular old sea dog!

TEMPLE: O'Hara?

SNOOKER: Yes. Maybe you know him?

TEMPLE: No. No, I can't say I do.

SNOOKER: He's a card! You'd like O'Hara. (*Laughing*) Captain Michael Shaun Dougherty O'Hara … Skipper of The Simon Lee …

TEMPLE: (*After a moment, dumbfounded*) The … Simon … Lee …?

SNOOKER: (*Surprised by TEMPLE's reaction*) Why, yes!

STEVE: (*Suddenly, realising that she has heard the name before*) But, Paul, that was the name that …

TEMPLE: (*Cutting in*) Snooker, tell me – how long have you known O'Hara?

SNOOKER: O'Hara? Oh – I've known O'Hara donkey's years. He's been skipper of The Simon Lee … (*Suddenly: suspicious*) Look 'ere, if you're interested in O'Hara, China – then O'Hara's the bloke you want to talk to!

TEMPLE: (*Pleasantly*) That's not a bad idea at that, Snooker. How can I get hold of him?

A moment.

SNOOKER: (*Cautiously*) Do you know The Marquis of Bude – it's a pub just off The Causeway, Limehouse?

TEMPLE: It's not exactly my favourite rendezvous – but I know it.

SNOOKER: I'll see you there tomorrow night …

TEMPLE: What time?

SNOOKER: (*After a moment's hesitation*) Nine o'clock.

TEMPLE: O.K. Nine o'clock. (*A pause*) With O'Hara …

36

SNOOKER: (*Watching TEMPLE; a slow nod*) With O'Hara
                …

FADE UP of MUSIC.

FADE DOWN of MUSIC.
FADE UP of noises of a crowded, rather rowdy, public bar.
The cash register can be heard.

STEVE: I don't see your friend Snooker.

TEMPLE: (*Staring round*) No. Perhaps we're a bit on the
            early side.

STEVE: Quite a salubrious crowd!

TEMPLE: Yes. Let's go and sit over there in the corner.
            (*Surprised*) Why, hello, Superintendent!

WETHERBY: (*Also surprised*) Hello, Mr Temple! I didn't
            expect to find you here, sir. (*Pleasantly*) Good
            evening, Mrs Temple.

TEMPLE: (*Lightly*) What are you doing here, Wetherby?
            This place is a bit off the beaten track for you,
            isn't it?

WETHERBY: Well, if it comes to that, what are you doing
            here, Mr Temple?

TEMPLE: Yes … (*With a little laugh*) Yes …

WETHERBY: (*Suddenly*) Oh – I'd like you to meet Mr
            Kelvin. Mr Kelvin – Mr and Mrs Temple.

KELVIN: How do you do?

STEVE: How do you do?

TEMPLE: (*Intrigued*) Mr Kelvin? That's rather
            interesting. As a matter of fact, we're hoping to
            meet quite a friend of yours here tonight, Mr
            Kelvin.

KELVIN: Oh – indeed?

TEMPLE: (*After a moment*) Snooker Riley …

KELVIN:	(*Puzzled*) Snooker Riley … (*Remembering*) Oh! Oh, that was the man I met last night on … on … the houseboat …
TEMPLE:	Yes …
KELVIN:	He's not a friend of mine, Mr Temple, I only … (*He checks himself; hesitates*)
WETHERBY:	It's all right, Kelvin, you can talk.
KELVIN:	(*With an effort: a strange tenseness in his voice*) Yesterday afternoon my wife committed suicide …
TEMPLE:	Yes …
KELVIN:	I suppose you read all about it in the newspapers. They made quite a story, didn't they? Quite an interesting story of how she jumped off … (*He controls himself; then in a cold, incisive manner*) She'd been taking drugs – cocaine …
TEMPLE:	Go on …
KELVIN:	The drugs were supplied by a man called Valentine. (*Quietly*) I'm going to get Valentine, Mr Temple; and when I do get him … (*Suddenly, completely losing control of himself*) When I do get my hands on the swine, I'll …
WETHERBY:	(*Quietly*) Steady, old man! Steady!
TEMPLE:	Is that why you saw Snooker Riley, because …
KELVIN:	I saw Snooker Riley because I'm convinced – quite convinced – that he's mixed up in this affair!
WETHERBY:	That's the trouble with all you amateur detectives! You pick on a nice unsuspecting little guy and before you know where you are, you've sold yourself the idea that he's the master criminal! Why Snooker Riley wouldn't … (*He breaks off*) What is it, Daisy?

DAISY: Are you Mr Temple?

WETHERBY: No. No, this is Mr Temple.

DAISY: Oh. Well – there's a gent upstairs. Say's he's got an appointment to see you.

TEMPLE: (*A moment*) Oh. Oh, thanks.

DAISY: Room 8. You'll see the door at the top of the landing.

TEMPLE: O.K.

WETHERBY: Would that be Snooker?

TEMPLE: (*Cautiously*) Could be. I think perhaps you'd better wait outside for me, darling, in the car – I shan't be very long.

STEVE: Yes, all right, Paul.

TEMPLE: I'll see you later, Wetherby.

WETHERBY: (*Pleasantly*) Yes, very good, Mr Temple. (*Fading*) If I can get near the bar, Kelvin, I'll buy you a drink, but …

FADE UP of bar parlour noises.

FADE to background.

TEMPLE is climbing the staircase.

Continue FADE of bar parlour noises.

TEMPLE arrives on the landing.

A door opens.

O'HARA: (*With gusto*) Come in! Ah, I've been expecting you! Come in!

The door closes.

TEMPLE: Captain O'Hara?

O'HARA: Captain O'Hara it is! Captain Michael Shaun Dougherty O'Hara; at your service, sir.

TEMPLE: Where's Snooker?

O'HARA: Mr Riley, I regret to say, was unavoidably detained. Cherchez la femme. (*Brightly*) Sit down! Sit down! Now what'll ye have?

TEMPLE: Do you usually engage a private sitting room, Captain O'Hara?

O'HARA: Well, now, it depends entirely on the company I'm expecting. Would you prefer that we talk downstairs so that your friend Superintendent Wetherby can hear the conversation?

TEMPLE: (*A moment*) We'll talk here, and I'll have a large whisky …

O'HARA: That's great. I can see you're a man after me own heart. (*Pours whisky*) Will ye be having it polluted or otherwise?

TEMPLE: Polluted, thank you.

The sound of a syphon.

A pause.

O'HARA: Now what can I do for you?

TEMPLE: Snooker tells me that you're skipper of The Simon Lee.

O'HARA: I am that. An' it's a fine boat, Mr Temple. A fine boat. Now if you're ever thinking of taking a cruise, I strongly advise …

TEMPLE: (*Cutting O'HARA short*) Captain O'Hara … (*A moment*) Have you ever heard of a man called … Valentine?

O'HARA: Valentine? Valentine, did ye say? (*Breezy; but not too convincing*) Why, it's a common enough name. As a matter of fact, I once knew a girl in San Diego called Valentine, an' a fine upstanding figure of a …

TEMPLE: I'm not talking about a girl in San Diego!

O'HARA: No?

TEMPLE: No.

O'HARA: Well, supposing you tell me exactly what it is you are talking about?

TEMPLE: (*Sharply*) I'm talking about opium, cocaine, heroin, amashyer …

O'HARA: Oh! (*Laughing*) Oh! Oh, I'm beginning to see daylight.

TEMPLE: (*With authority*) Scotland Yard have proof, definite proof, that there exists in the West End of London an organisation: a secret organisation dealing in dangerous drugs. The leader of that organisation is a man – (*Afterthought*) or woman – known as Valentine. (*Trying to throw a scare on O'HARA*) I have reason to believe, O'Hara, that you have been in contact with Valentine. If not in direct contact, then quite possibly …

O'HARA: (*Interrupting: a note of anger in his voice*) You've no reason to believe anything of the sort, man – an' well you know it! You're guessing!

A pause.

TEMPLE: (*Pleasantly, and quite simply*) You're quite right, Captain O'Hara, I'm guessing.

O'HARA: (*Laughs*) Mr Temple, supposing now I talked quite freely, man to man as you might say; would it be off the record?

TEMPLE: Quite off the record.

O'HARA: I have your assurance on that point?

TEMPLE: You have my assurance.

O'HARA: I wouldn't stand to lose anything by it, I mean …

TEMPLE: What you really mean is – would you stand to gain? The answer is yes – to the tune of a pony.

O'HARA: A pony …

TEMPLE: A pony is twenty-five pounds, Captain O'Hara. Satisfactory?

O'HARA: I'm thinking it's an infinitesimal sum to offer a man of my standing, Mr Temple, but however (*A moment*) Two months ago, just as I was on the point of leaving for Amsterdam, I received a telephone message from a man who called himself Sir Gilbert

41

Dryden. He asked me to deliver a letter to a woman in Amsterdam. In return for the letter, I was to receive a parcel. I was told to bring the parcel back to England and to deliver it myself – personally – to an address in Bloomsbury.

TEMPLE: You delivered the parcel?

O'HARA: I did.

TEMPLE: What was in it?

O'HARA: I don't know. It was an ordinary – quite small – brown paper parcel.

TEMPLE: Was it addressed to Sir Gilbert Dryden?

O'HARA: (*After a significant hesitation*) No.

TEMPLE: Who was it addressed to?

O'HARA: Well, for the life of me, I just can't think!

TEMPLE: (*Sharply*) Who was it addressed to?

O'HARA: It was addressed to … Mr Valentine.

TEMPLE: When you delivered the parcel did you see anyone at the house or …

O'HARA: A servant. I simply handed over the parcel to her, and she – she gave me an envelope.

TEMPLE: You expected the envelope?

O'HARA: I did that!

TEMPLE: How much?

O'HARA: Two – two hundred quid.

TEMPLE: M'm. Not bad. Not bad, O'Hara. (*A moment*) Was this the first time that anything like that had happened or …

O'HARA: The first time! The first an' the last, Mr Temple – I swear it!

TEMPLE: You've not heard from Sir Gilbert Dryden since?

O'HARA: No.

TEMPLE: (*A moment*) What was the address in Bloomsbury?

O'HARA: I don't … (*Changing his mind*) … The address was Four hundred and Seventy-nine Estonia Avenue.

TEMPLE: Four – Seventy-nine – Estonia Avenue …?

O'HARA: Yes …

TEMPLE: (*A moment*) You say, you don't know what was in the parcel?

O'HARA: No. (*Faintly amused*) But I think I can guess …

TEMPLE: (*Quietly; significantly*) I think we can both guess, O'Hara … Tell me: where were you when you received the message from Sir Gilbert?

O'HARA: I was in a pub – The Golden Horse, it's right on the corner …

TEMPLE: Yes, I know it. Did you give him a definite answer there and then?

O'HARA: I did that! I told him he could go to blazes!

TEMPLE: But you changed your mind apparently?

O'HARA: Yes, I … changed … my mind.

TEMPLE: (*Quietly; terminating the interview*) O.K., O'Hara. O.K. Four hundred and seventy-nine, you say?

O'HARA: That's right … Four seventy-nine, Estonia Avenue … you can't mistake the house, Mr Temple … You can't mistake it.

FADE UP of MUSIC.

FADE DOWN of MUSIC.
A car drives to a standstill, and we hear the opening and closing of a car door.

STEVE: Well, this is the house, darling.

TEMPLE: Yes, it looks very much like it. Four … Seventy … Nine … Yes, this is it, all right. Not particularly impressive, is it?

STEVE: There's a plate of some sort on the gate, Paul. It looks to me as if …

TEMPLE: (*Reading*) Robert Y. Frobisher, Dental Surgeon …

STEVE: (*Surprised*) Dental surgeon!

TEMPLE: M'm. (*He opens the gate*) By Timothy, just look at the garden! They've got some pretty snappy weeds around here!

TEMPLE and STEVE walk up the path.

STEVE: Here's the bell, darling.

TEMPLE pulls the bell: it is an old-fashioned spring-pull bell. It can be heard in the house.

A pause.

STEVE: There doesn't seem to be anyone in!

TEMPLE pulls the bell again.

Another pause.

STEVE: They're certainly not hurrying themselves!

TEMPLE: It's a good job we're not howling our heads off with toothache.

STEVE: Try again!

TEMPLE: If at first you don't succeed try … (*He stops: a little laugh*) There's no need to try again …

STEVE: What do you mean, darling?

TEMPLE: Look! The door's open! (*He pushes open the door*)

STEVE: Good heavens, so it is! (*Quickly*) Paul, what are you going to do?

TEMPLE: (*Matter of fact*) Don't be silly, Steve – what do you think I'm going to do?

STEVE: (*Nervously*) The last time …

TEMPLE: I know! I know! I know what you're thinking! Mrs Trevelyan and Marshall House Terrace … But this is different, darling. O'Hara didn't send me here, he simply … (*Hesitates; quietly*) Hello, what's this?

STEVE: What is it?

TEMPLE: It's … just … a … letter I noticed on the mat, it … (*He picks up the letter*) Hello, that's interesting …

STEVE: (*Reading*) Sir Gilbert Dryden, care of …

TEMPLE: (*Reading*) … care of Four Seventy-Nine … Estonia Avenue … Bloomsbury …

STEVE: (*Quickly*) That was the man O'Hara told you about
           …

TEMPLE: (*Interrupting STEVE*) Yes! (*Quietly*) I wonder if
           there's anyone in this house, Steve …

STEVE: (*Nervously*) Well, there must be someone here,
           darling, otherwise …

TEMPLE: Would you like to wait in the car while I …

STEVE: No … No … I'll stay with you!

TEMPLE: O.K. – we'll see what happens, anyway. (*Raising
           his voice*) Hello! Hello there! Anybody at home?!!!
           (*Pause*) M'm … (*Shouts again*) Hello, there!!!!
           (*Angry note*) Anybody at home?!!!

STEVE laughs.

STEVE: Darling, you needn't sound so aggressive!

TEMPLE laughs.

TEMPLE: What's this place over here …?

STEVE: (*Away from TEMPLE*) I should think that's a
           cloakroom … Here's the door to the surgery, Paul
           … (*She opens the door, gives a sudden, stifled gasp
           of astonishment, and closes it*)

TEMPLE: (*Quickly*) What is it? What's the matter?

STEVE: (*Softly; frightened*) There's – there's someone in
           there … sitting in the chair …

TEMPLE: Don't be silly, darling, there can't be, he'd have
           heard us.

STEVE: (*Tensely; frightened*) I tell you I saw him! He's in
           the chair! He's in the dentist's chair sitting in front
           of the window …

TEMPLE: But, Steve, he'd have heard me shouting, he …

STEVE: Darling, I saw him! I saw him! Honestly, he …

TEMPLE: All right … Wait a minute!!! (*He throws open the
           surgery door*)

STEVE: (*Softly*) There you are …

TEMPLE: (*Quite pleasantly*) Oh, I beg your pardon, sir! My wife and I happened to … to … to …

STEVE: What is it? What's the matter with him?

TEMPLE: (*Quietly*) I think you'd better go outside, darling …

STEVE: (*Suddenly; aghast*) Oh, Paul, look!!!! (*Horrified*) Look!!! Look at his throat, he … Paul!!!! (*She is approaching hysteria*) Paul, he's been murdered!!!

TEMPLE: (*With authority*) Steve!!! Pull yourself together!!! (*A moment: STEVE is sobbing slightly*) Steve!!!

STEVE: I'm … I'm sorry, darling. I'm ... all right … now.

TEMPLE: (*Quietly*) Wait here, by the door.

A pause.

STEVE: He's … dead …?

TEMPLE: Yes …

STEVE: What's that your holding – that card …?

Another pause.

TEMPLE: It was on the chair …

STEVE: What does it say? (*Anxiously; frightened again*) Paul, what does it say?

TEMPLE: (*After a moment: slowly, deep in thought*) It says … "Permit me to introduce the REAL Captain O'Hara. Let this be a warning Mr Temple and do not interfere … Valentine" …

Quick FADE UP of MUSIC.

The music quickly reaches a climax.

A door opens.

MARY: Good evening to you both – I'm glad you're back because you've got visitors.

STEVE: Visitors?

MARY: Yes, Sir Graham Forbes and another man called Major Peters.

TEMPLE: Oh, good! Thank you, Mary.

MARY: Not at all.

46

A second door opens.

SIR GRAHAM is talking to MAJOR PETERS, and he stops as the door opens.

FORBES: Hello, Temple!

TEMPLE: You're just the man I want to see, Sir Graham!

PETERS: You're just the man <u>we</u> want to see, Mr Temple.

TEMPLE: (*Curious: noting their expression*) Oh? Why?

FORBES: Temple, have you heard of a man called Sir Gilbert Dryden?

TEMPLE: Sir Gil ... (*Surprised; but with a laugh*) What is this – a joke?

STEVE: (*Astonished*) Of course we've heard of Sir Gilbert Dryden, why only tonight ...

TEMPLE: (*Quickly*) What is it? What's happened?

FORBES: (*After a moment; quietly; seriously*) All right, Peters – read the letter ...

PETERS: This letter was delivered to Scotland Yard by special messenger just after eight o'clock tonight. It was addressed to Sir Graham and was marked 'Personal' and 'Urgent'. "Dear Sir ... With reference to the Valentine case. I know the identity of Valentine and have conveyed this important information to a man called Snooker Riley. Riley will meet you tonight shortly before midnight, at Dellford Quarry, Kempton Heath ... Respectfully yours, ... Sir Gilbert Dryden ..."

TEMPLE: M'm – that sounds a phoney to me ...

FORBES: That's what I said, but Peters ...

PETERS: I'm not so sure, Temple, in any case, we can't afford to ignore it.

STEVE: Where is Dellford Quarry, Kempton Heath ...?

FORBES: It's about four or five miles the other side of Kempton.

PETERS: Wetherby should be there by now, sir.

47

FORBES:	Yes.
TEMPLE:	Wetherby?
FORBES:	I've got Superintendent Wetherby and two of the Flying Squad units on the job.
TEMPLE:	But we saw Wetherby about an hour ago, he was in a pub called The Marquis of Bude.
FORBES:	Yes, he went there to meet a young man called Charles Kelvin. Kelvin's wife committed suicide yesterday afternoon and I'm rather afraid the poor devil fancies himself as a sort of amateur detective!
PETERS:	(*Faintly amused*) He's certainly worrying the life out of poor old Wetherby.
FORBES:	(*Suddenly curious*) You say you've heard of this man Sir Gilbert Dryden?
TEMPLE:	Yes, as a matter of fact I heard of him tonight for the … (*The clock in the hall is chiming*) But look here, are we supposed to be going to Kempton Heath, because …
FORBES:	Yes …
TEMPLE:	O.K.! I'll tell you all about it on the way there. (*Briskly*) Cheerio, darling, we shan't be very long!
STEVE:	(*Anxiously*) Take care!
TEMPLE:	Yes, of course! Don't worry! We'll be back in about an hour and a half all being well …

FADE UP of MUSIC.

FADE DOWN of MUSIC.

FADE IN a car: it is heard travelling in from the distance and slowly comes to a standstill. The car door opens.

Pause.

PETERS:	Dellford Quarry! (*Shivers*) Brr! Not exactly my idea of a health resort!

48

FORBES: I wonder if that's Wetherby over there …
             (*Shouting*) Is that you, Wetherby?
TEMPLE: (*After a moment*) I think it is …
Slight pause.
SUPERINTENDENT WETHERBY arrives.
WETHERBY: Hello, Peters! Oh, good evening, sir!
FORBES: Well, have you seen anyone?
WETHERBY: No … No, sir; not a soul.
TEMPLE: Good evening, Superintendent!
WETHERBY: (*Taken aback*) Oh! Oh, good evening, Mr
             Temple – I didn't recognise you, sir. This is a
             surprise, sir!
TEMPLE: Yes, isn't it?
PETERS: Which way do you think Riley will come?
WETHERBY: (*Extremely dubious*) Well, if he comes, it's my
             bet that … (*Stops*) What is it?
TEMPLE: (*Quietly, casually*) I thought I heard something
             …
A pause.
FORBES: No …
PETERS: No, I don't think so …
WETHERBY: You can imagine all sorts of noises if once you
             allow your imagination to run away.
TEMPLE: Sh!
A pause.
TEMPLE: Didn't you hear that?
PETERS: What?
TEMPLE: Listen …
Another pause.
FORBES: (*Faintly annoyed*) I'm damned if I can hear
             anything!
TEMPLE: You will, Sir Graham! Listen!!!
FORBES: (*After another pause*) Well, I may be deaf but
             … (*He hesitates*)

49

There is another pause, then from the background can be heard a sort of low moan. It is the final cry of a man who has suffered great pain.

PETERS: Ye Gods, I heard that all right!!!

FORBES: Quiet!!! Sh!!!

Pause.

We hear the cry again.

PETERS: It's near that tree over on the right! I'll swear it is!

WETHERBY: But I've just come from there! I never saw anyone!

TEMPLE: No, you probably wouldn't, not if he was right up against the tree!

PETERS: (*Quickly, tensely*) Give me that torch, Wetherby … Quickly!!!

A moment: PETERS clicks on the torch.

WETHERBY: Look! There he is!

PETERS: You were right, Temple!

WETHERBY: He's been stabbed, Peters. Look – you can see!

FORBES: Wetherby, what's that on the ground near your foot?

WETHERBY: It's the knife, sir.

FORBES: Don't touch it!

TEMPLE: Here – here's my handkerchief!

FORBES: (*Softly*) Do you recognise him, Temple?

TEMPLE: (Quietly) Yes … It's Snooker Riley …

FADE UP of MUSIC.

FADE DOWN of MUSIC.

We hear a latch key in a lock: a door opens.

TEMPLE: Oh, hello, Mary. I thought you'd be in bed by now!

MARY:	I was just having a wee cup of coffee – I'm awfully partial to coffee. I'll make some more if you'd like some.
TEMPLE:	Very much, yes! Where's Mrs Temple?
MARY:	In the lounge. I'll be along with the coffee in two shakes of a lamb's tail.
TEMPLE:	(*A little laugh; he is feeling tired*) Thank you, Mary.
MARY:	Not at all. You're welcome.

TEMPLE opens the lounge door.

STEVE:	Oh, hello, Paul! You look tired …

The door closes.

TEMPLE:	Yes, I feel tired. By Timothy, what a night! (*Rather surprised*) Good Lord, is it a quarter past one?
STEVE:	Yes.
TEMPLE:	You should have gone to bed, Steve.
STEVE:	Mary's making some coffee.
TEMPLE:	Yes, I know, and by Timothy, I can use it.
STEVE:	Did you see Snooker Riley?
TEMPLE:	(*A moment*) Yes, Steve.
STEVE:	What happened?
TEMPLE:	Well … (*He hesitates*)
STEVE:	You'd rather not talk about it?
TEMPLE:	It isn't that, only … (*He hesitates again*)
STEVE:	(*Simply, yet worried*) What's going to happen, darling, about – about this business?
TEMPLE:	(*A moment; simply*) I'm going to catch Valentine. (*Suddenly*) Oh, Steve, I know how you feel about my getting … (*He is interrupted by the telephone; it continues for a moment*) I wonder who that is?
STEVE:	I don't know. (*A slight pause*) It's very late, darling …

TEMPLE: Yes … It's all right, I'll take it.

TEMPLE lifts the receiver.

TEMPLE: (*On the phone*) Hello?

SHEILA: (*On the other end of the phone; quickly*) Hello – Mr Temple?

TEMPLE: Yes.

SHEILA: (*Quickly, tensely*) I don't know whether you remember, Mr Temple, but I telephoned you last night. My name …

TEMPLE: (*Significantly*) Oh, yes. I remember … Miss Baxter … Miss Sheila Baxter.

SHEILA: Mr Temple, don't … (*With an effort*) … don't … believe a word he tells you … it isn't true … it isn't true … any of it.

TEMPLE: What do you mean? I say, who are you talking about, I …

SHEILA: I'm – I'm talking about Dryden … Don't believe him, Mr Temple, please – please don't believe him …

TEMPLE: But how can I believe him, I haven't even …

SHEILA has replaced the receiver.

TEMPLE: … Hello! Hello! … (*Quietly, after a moment*) She's rung off … (*He replaces the receiver: a tiny pause*) Did you hear that?

STEVE: Yes.

TEMPLE: All of it?

STEVE: I – I think so. (*Puzzled*) But what does it mean, Paul, I – I … just can't …

The lounge door is thrown open. Voices are heard.

TEMPLE: (*Sharply, annoyed*) What is it, Mary?

MARY: (*Faintly perturbed*) I'm awfully sorry, Mr Temple, but this gentleman insisted on …

DRYDEN: I'm so sorry to intrude, but – may I come in? (*A silence*) My name is Dryden. (*Excessively polite*) Sir Gilbert Dryden …
FADE UP of MUSIC.

END OF EPISODE TWO

EPISODE THREE

IN WHICH
SIR GILBERT EXPLAINS

OPEN TO:

ANNOUNCER: Paul Temple, the celebrated novelist and private detective, is visited by an old friend, Sir Graham Forbes, the Chief Commissioner of Scotland Yard, and by a Major Peters who is attached to the Special Branch of the Criminal Investigation Department. Sir Graham tells Temple that for the past three months …

Quick FADE UP of SIR GRAHAM.

FORBES: For the past three months, Major Peters, Superintendent Wetherby and myself, have been investigating a case known to us at Scotland Yard as The Granger Affair. Three months ago, a girl called Lesley Granger committed suicide. There was an inquest, and it was discovered that Lesley Granger had been taking drugs – cocaine. She had been getting the cocaine presumably from a secret source. From a man – or woman – known to her quite simply as – Valentine.

TEMPLE: Valentine? Sir Graham, are you suggesting …

FORBES: I'm suggesting that there exists in the West End of London, at the present moment, a secret organisation trafficking exclusively in dangerous drugs. That organisation is growing, Temple. It's growing so rapidly that unless we can put our fingers on the person who controls it – unless we can find the …

PETERS: (*Ominously*) Unless we can find this mysterious Mr Valentine, there's going to be a new crime wave in this country: a crime wave quite without precedent.

57

FORBES:	Believe me, that's no exaggeration!
PETERS:	Early this evening, Superintendent Wetherby interviewed a young man called Charles Kelvin …
FORBES:	… He's the husband of the girl that committed suicide this afternoon – as a matter of fact he identified the body.
TEMPLE:	Yes …
PETERS:	During the course of cross examination, Kelvin admitted that his wife had been – difficult – highly strung – emotional. On two occasions – during a hysterical outburst – he remembers quite distinctly that she repeated the name Simon Lee.
TEMPLE:	Did the name have any particular significance, so far as Kelvin himself was concerned?
PETERS:	No. He's just as puzzled as we are. He's never even heard of anyone called Simon Lee.
TEMPLE:	M'm. Well – er – what do you want me to do exactly?
PETERS:	Don't you know? (*A moment; quietly*) We want you to catch Valentine, Mr Temple.

A moment, then TEMPLE starts to laugh.
FADE laugh out.

ANNOUNCER:	During the course of the same evening, Temple receives a telephone message from a mysterious girl who introduces herself as Sheila Baxter. Later, Paul Temple, together with Steve, his wife, visit Snooker Riley. Snooker, a strange, rather disreputable little cockney, informs Temple that a friend of his – a certain Captain O'Hara – is the skipper of

... The Simon Lee. The following evening Temple is informed by O'Hara that ...

FADE UP of O'HARA.

O'HARA: Two months ago, just as I was on the point of leaving for Amsterdam, I received a telephone message from a man who called himself Sir Gilbert Dryden. He asked me to deliver a letter to a woman in Amsterdam. In return for the letter, I was to receive a parcel. I was told to bring the parcel back to England and to deliver it myself – personally – to an address in Bloomsbury.

TEMPLE: What was the address?

O'HARA: I don't ... (*Changing his mind*) ... The address was Four hundred and Seventy-nine Estonia Avenue.

TEMPLE: Four – Seventy-nine – Estonia Avenue ...?

O'HARA: Yes ...

FADE UP of ANNOUNCER.

ANNOUNCER: But when Temple and Steve arrive at Four hundred and Seventy-nine Estonia Avenue, they discover to their astonishment the dead body of the REAL Captain O'Hara. Later the same night, after a visit to Dellford Quarry with Sir Graham Forbes and Major Peters, Temple returns to his flat ...

Quick flourish of music.

FADE MUSIC DOWN.
We hear a latch key in a lock: a door opens.
TEMPLE: Oh, hello, Mary. I thought you'd be in bed by now!

MARY: I was just having a wee cup of coffee – I'm awfully partial to coffee. I'll make some more if you'd like some.

TEMPLE: Very much, yes! Where's Mrs Temple?

MARY: In the lounge. I'll be along with the coffee in two shakes of a lamb's tail.

TEMPLE: (*A little laugh; he is feeling tired*) Thank you, Mary.

MARY: Not at all. You're welcome.

TEMPLE opens the lounge door.

STEVE: Oh, hello, Paul! You look tired …

The door closes.

TEMPLE: Yes, I feel tired. By Timothy, what a night! (*Rather surprised*) Good Lord, is it a quarter past one?

STEVE: Yes.

TEMPLE: You should have gone to bed, Steve.

STEVE: Mary's making some coffee.

TEMPLE: Yes, I know, and by Timothy, I can use it.

STEVE: Did you see Snooker Riley?

TEMPLE: (*A moment*) Yes, Steve.

STEVE: What happened?

TEMPLE: Well … (*He hesitates*)

STEVE: You'd rather not talk about it?

TEMPLE: It isn't that, only … (*He hesitates again*)

STEVE: (*Simply, yet worried*) What's going to happen, darling, about – about this business?

TEMPLE: (*A moment; simply*) I'm going to catch Valentine. (*Suddenly*) Oh, Steve, I know how you feel about my getting … (*He is interrupted by the telephone; it continues for a moment*) I wonder who that is?

STEVE: I don't know. (*A slight pause*) It's very late, darling …

TEMPLE: Yes … It's all right, I'll take it.

TEMPLE lifts the receiver.

TEMPLE: (*On the phone*) Hello?

SHEILA: (*On the other end of the phone; quickly*) Hello – Mr Temple?

TEMPLE: Yes.

SHEILA: (*Quickly, tensely*) I don't know whether you remember, Mr Temple, but I telephoned you last night. My name …

TEMPLE: (*Significantly*) Oh, yes. I remember … Miss Baxter … Miss Sheila Baxter.

SHEILA: Mr Temple, don't … (*With an effort*) … don't … believe a word he tells you … it isn't true … it isn't true … any of it.

TEMPLE: What do you mean? I say, who are you talking about, I …

SHEILA: I'm – I'm talking about Dryden … Don't believe him, Mr Temple, please – please don't believe him …

TEMPLE: But how can I believe him, I haven't even …

SHEILA has replaced the receiver.

TEMPLE: … Hello! Hello! … (*Quietly, after a moment*) She's rung off … (*He replaces the receiver: a tiny pause*) Did you hear that?

STEVE: Yes.

TEMPLE: All of it?

STEVE: I – I think so. (*Puzzled*) But what does it mean, Paul, I – I … just can't …

The lounge door is thrown open. Voices are heard.

TEMPLE: (*Sharply, annoyed*) What is it, Mary?

MARY: (*Faintly perturbed*) I'm awfully sorry, Mr Temple, but this gentleman insisted on …

DRYDEN: I'm so sorry to intrude, but – may I come in? (*A silence*) My name is Dryden. (*Excessively polite*) Sir Gilbert Dryden …

STEVE gives a little cry of astonishment.

TEMPLE: (*Quietly; after a moment*) That's all right, Mary …
you can close the door.

MARY: The very idea – barging in like that!

MARY goes, closing the door behind her.

DRYDEN: You must forgive me for calling at this – at this
unearthly hour, Mr Temple, but the matter is, I
assure you, of some importance.

TEMPLE: Indeed?

DRYDEN: Since I don't suppose you've actually heard of me,
Mr Temple, I would like …

TEMPLE: On the contrary, Sir Gilbert – I appear to be coming
across your name with monotonous regularity.

DRYDEN: (*Puzzled*) What – what do you mean, sir?

TEMPLE: (*Quietly: testing the reaction*) I was thinking of your
friend Captain O'Hara at … Four hundred and
Seventy-nine Estonia Avenue …

DRYDEN: (*Apparently completely bewildered*) Captain
O'Hara?

TEMPLE: I take it you've never heard of Captain O'Hara?

DRYDEN: I most certainly have not, sir! (*Suddenly*) Mr
Temple, why do you think I came to see you this
evening?

TEMPLE: I don't know. Why did you come to see me, Sir
Gilbert?

DRYDEN: (*Suddenly, his self-confidence falling from him; he
is a very worried man*) Because I'm worried –
desperately – terribly worried. I need your help, Mr
Temple … I need your help … and if … (*He
hesitates*)

TEMPLE: If what?

DRYDEN: If you'll do what I want, sir – if you'll do precisely
what I want, I'll … (*A definite decision*) … I'll pay
you fifteen hundred pounds.

TEMPLE: Fifteen hundred pounds? Fifteen hundred pounds is a lot of money, Sir Gilbert. What – er – precisely would you like me to do for your fifteen hundred pounds?

DRYDEN: You have a reputation, sir, one might almost say an international reputation, as a private investigator. I want you to undertake certain private, er – highly confidential, investigations …

TEMPLE: (*After a moment*) What exactly would be the nature of these investigations?

DRYDEN: Mr Temple, many years ago, a friend of mine died and left an only child. I adopted that child. I sent her to college, to finishing school, I … well … I gave her literally everything that money could buy. When she reached the age of twenty-one, she decided that she wanted to open a beauty parlour in Brussels. I agreed to finance the proposition, and in the spring of 1933, she opened a tiny, but quite exclusive, little shop in the Rue Raspelier. I saw very little of her during the next two or three years, although we corresponded fairly frequently, and I continued to send her the usual monthly allowance. But in 1938, rather to my surprise, she came to London and opened a beauty parlour in Mayfair. I was delighted by this move because I thought, not unnaturally, that we should see a great deal of each other. But she'd changed, Mr Temple. The gentle, quiet, rather unsophisticated child had changed. In her place, there was a strange, metallic kind of person … (*Quickly*) Don't misunderstand me, outwardly she was just the same – charming, attractive – but inwardly something … had happened …

TEMPLE: Go on …

DRYDEN: We went to the theatre together, we dined together, we appeared – as I say, outwardly – to be quite good friends. Then suddenly, about twelve months ago, I began to have my suspicions. I can't tell you how it happened – or why it happened – but I began to suspect that she was mixed up in something. Something that was not quite – how can I put it? – not quite above board.

STEVE: (*Quietly; intensely interested*) What do you suspect, Sir Gilbert?

A pause.

DRYDEN: (*Slowly, seriously*) I suspect that she is the leader of an organisation dealing drugs. I suspect that she is … Valentine.

STEVE: Valentine?

TEMPLE: Her name?

DRYDEN: Well, professionally, she's known as Madame De Briac, but …

STEVE: (*Surprised*) Madame De Briac! But I know the shop! It's on Curzon Street!

DRYDEN: Yes. But her real name is Sheila Baxter …

TEMPLE: You offered me fifteen hundred pounds, Sir Gilbert. Why?

DRYDEN: (*Interrupting TEMPLE: with a return to his previous manner*) I want you to discover whether my suspicions are justified – or not. If what I suspect is true, and she is Valentine, then I should want you to give me your assurance, Mr Temple, that before you place your information at the disposal of the police, she …

TEMPLE: She would have ample opportunity of leaving for – shall we say – South America?

A moment.

DRYDEN: You decline my offer?

TEMPLE: Most decidedly …

DRYDEN: Then there's nothing more to be said …

TEMPLE: On the contrary, Sir Gilbert! On the contrary! Last night, during the course of certain investigations, I made the acquaintance of a man who called himself Captain O'Hara. Captain O'Hara informed me that he was the skipper of a cargo boat knows as The Simon Lee. (*Politely*) You've never heard of The Simon Lee, I take it?

DRYDEN: I've already told you, sir, I've never heard of Captain O'Hara, so it's highly unlikely that I should have heard of The Simon …

TEMPLE: Lee. However: Captain O'Hara told me that two months ago he received a telephone message from you …

DRYDEN: (*Astounded*) From me!

TEMPLE: From you, sir … asking him to deliver a letter to a woman in Amsterdam. In return for the letter, Captain O'Hara received a parcel which he delivered to an address in Bloomsbury. The address was Four hundred and Seventy-nine Estonia Avenue.

DRYDEN: (*Bewildered*) But this is absurd!

TEMPLE: After our interesting chat with the – er – so called Captain O'Hara, my wife and I visited Estonia Avenue. (*A moment; seriously*) Not only did we find the dead body of the real Captain O'Hara but … we found this letter – it was on the mat just inside the hall.

DRYDEN: What – what letter?

TEMPLE: This letter – addressed to Sir Gilbert Dryden …

DRYDEN: (*Suddenly worried and completely bewildered*) Mr Temple, I assure you I've never heard of Captain O'Hara … I know nothing … Nothing whatsoever

about a house in … in … Estonia Avenue …
(*Quickly*) What does it say? What does the letter
say?

TEMPLE: (*Quietly*) It's addressed to you, Sir Gilbert …

DRYDEN: But open it, sir … Open it …

TEMPLE tears the letter open.

A pause.

DRYDEN: Well?

TEMPLE: Read it for yourself …

DRYDEN:(*Reading, nervously*) "The package you are
expecting will arrive on the 22nd. Meet me, as
arranged, on the houseboat. I shall be there by
eleven … Valentine" …

STEVE: The 22nd! That's tomorrow …

TEMPLE: Today, darling, it's after midnight …

DRYDEN:(*Still apparently bewildered*) But what houseboat?
What does he mean by … the package that you are
expecting …? I'm not expecting a package, I … Mr
Temple, what does it all mean?

TEMPLE: Sir Gilbert, tell me; did you write to Scotland Yard
about a man called Snooker Riley?

DRYDEN: Why – why, no! I've never heard of a man called
Snooker Riley …

TEMPLE: I see. (*A moment, then*) Sir Gilbert, would you like
me to give you a piece of advice? Forget that you've
ever seen or even heard of this letter, and just …
wait …

DRYDEN:Wait? But – supposing my suspicions about Sheila
are true …

TEMPLE: If your suspicions about Madame De Briac are true,
there's nothing you can do about it.

DRYDEN:Yes … Yes, perhaps you're right … (*Thoughtfully*)
But you know, Mr Temple, I'm not sure that you
haven't put rather a different complexion on things

66

... In view of what you've told me tonight, in view of your most extraordinary story about the mysterious Captain O'Hara and the house in Estonia Avenue, I feel ...

TEMPLE: Yes?

DRYDEN: I feel that I might perhaps have been a little over hasty in – in jumping to conclusions – about ... Sheila.

TEMPLE: In short, you're no longer convinced that she's Valentine?

DRYDEN: Well – I'm certainly beginning to think that there are other possibilities. You see, whoever Valentine is, he – or she, of course – is obviously intent upon throwing suspicion on to ...

TEMPLE: On to yourself ...?

DRYDEN: Yes. And Sheila wouldn't do that. She's changed, I know; changed in a hundred and one ways, but – I'm sure she wouldn't do that.

TEMPLE: (*Dismissing DRYDEN*) Well, you have my assurance that this interview will be treated in the strictest confidence, Sir Gilbert.

DRYDEN: Thank you, sir. Well – goodnight, Mrs Temple. I – I hope that we shall meet again under slightly pleasanter circumstances.

TEMPLE: I hope so too, Sir Gilbert ...

DRYDEN: (*Departing*) There's no need to show me out, Mr Temple. I expect I shall be able to find ... (*FADE away*)

A door opens.

Pause.

Door opens and closes.

STEVE: Well, what do you think of Sir Gilbert Dryden?

TEMPLE: I think ... (*Suddenly; a change of thought*) I think I'd like to have another look at him.

STEVE: What do you mean?

TEMPLE: Put the light out and come over to the window …

TEMPLE draws back the curtains.

A pause.

TEMPLE: There he goes …

TEMPLE: Yes …

STEVE: It's an awfully nice car, isn't it?

TEMPLE: (*Quietly*) Yes …

STEVE: What are you looking at?

TEMPLE: I'm just looking at that car over on the other side of the road, it looks to me as if … as if … Yes, I thought so! He's been waiting for him … Look! Look!! He's going to tail him!

STEVE: Who is it? Can you see?

TEMPLE: No … No, can you?

STEVE: It's a man, darling, but I can't see what he looks like …

TEMPLE: (*Quickly*) What's the number?

STEVE: I think it's G M T 678.

TEMPLE: (*Quietly*) Yes … G M T 678 …

STEVE: Can you trace it?

TEMPLE: Yes, that ought to be simple. I'll have a word with Superintendent Wetherby in the morning.

STEVE: Draw the curtains, darling.

TEMPLE draws the curtains.

TEMPLE: (*A yawn*) Well, I don't know about you but I'm ready for bed. (*Casually*) Your hair doesn't look so good tonight, darling.

STEVE: What's the matter with it?

TEMPLE: (*Vaguely; off-hand*) Oh, I don't know; it just doesn't look so good …

STEVE: It could do with a perm, I suppose …

TEMPLE: Yes, I should get it done in the morning.

STEVE: Darling, you can't get it done in five minutes, you've got to make an appointment.

TEMPLE: Well, make an appointment!

STEVE: (*A moment; significantly*) At Madame De Briac's?

A tiny pause.

TEMPLE starts to laugh, a little self-consciously. STEVE joins in, her laugh indicates a "Yes, I know what you are up to!"

STEVE: I can read you like a book!

TEMPLE: That's because I'm a plain type, my sweet! Whoo!!

TEMPLE and STEVE laugh.

Quick FADE IN of MUSIC.

FADE DOWN of MUSIC.

Slight background of chatter.

STEVE: Good morning, I have an appointment for a permanent wave …

GIRL: (*A little too refined*) What name, Madam?

STEVE: Mrs Temple … It was a cancellation for half past eleven …

GIRL: (*Suddenly; remembering*) Oh, yes! Yes, I remember, Madam, of course! Please excuse me … (*She lifts the telephone receiver and dials*) I shan't keep you a moment, Madam … (*Into the phone*) Mrs Temple is here, Madame De Briac – yes, she's just arrived … Very good, Madame … (*Replaces the receiver*) Madame De Briac will be down in a moment, Mrs Temple – if you don't mind taking a seat …

STEVE: Thank you …

GIRL: (*Brightly*) Isn't the weather wretched for the time of the year? Still, I suppose one mustn't grumble, must one?

STEVE: I suppose one mustn't …

GIRL: (*Recognising SHEILA*) Ah, here's Madame De
          Briac …
SHEILA: (*Pleasantly*) Good morning – Mrs Temple?
STEVE: Yes.
SHEILA: My name is Madame De Briac. I don't think we've
          had the pleasure of …
STEVE: (*Interrupting SHEILA*) No, your name was
          mentioned to me by Edith Carstairs, and I thought
          …
SHEILA: Ah, yes, Mrs Carstairs! She's quite an old friend of
          ours. Would you mind stepping this way, Mrs
          Temple?
STEVE: Thank you.
SHEILA: Carol, tell Charles I'd like to see him – in my office.
GIRL: Certainly, Madame.
FADE DOWN of background noises.
A door opens.
SHEILA: Here we are, Mrs Temple … Do sit down …
STEVE: (*Impressed*) What a lovely office!
SHEILA: Yes, I brought a lot of the stuff over from the
          Continent with me when … No, sit over here near
          the window …
STEVE: Mrs Carstairs told me to ask for André …
SHEILA: I'm afraid André's on holiday just at the moment,
          but we've got a new man who is really most
          awfully good … (*She is faintly nervous, although
          extremely pleasant*) Will you have a cigarette?
STEVE: Not just at the moment, thank you …
SHEILA: I thought perhaps it might be quite a good idea if
          … if we had a little chat, Mrs Temple, before …
STEVE: (*Quietly*) I take it, my telephone call this morning
          was not entirely unexpected?
SHEILA: (*Slightly relieved*) Well – quite frankly – no. I
          thought something like this might happen,

especially after your visit last night from Sir Gilbert ... (*A shade amused*) You don't have to have a permanent wave, Mrs Temple, if you don't want one.

STEVE: My husband would never forgive me if I didn't have one.

SHEILA: But that's not why you came to see me?

STEVE: Not entirely.

SHEILA: I've behaved rather stupidly over this business. I don't know why I didn't ring your husband and talk to him quite frankly about the whole affair, but ... (*Suddenly*) Mrs Temple, I don't know what Sir Gilbert told your husband last night, but ... please ... please, whatever it was, ask Mr Temple to remember that there are always two sides to every story.

STEVE: (*Quietly*) That's why I'm here this morning, Madame De Briac, to hear your side of the story.

SHEILA: (*After a moment, with sincerity*) When I was a child my parents died, as a result of a motor car accident, and I was adopted by Sir Gilbert Dryden. I ... expect he told you that?

STEVE: Yes.

SHEILA: In those days Sir Gilbert was sweet and kind and generous. I really can't speak too highly, Mrs Temple, of ... of the hundred and one things he did for me. When I left finishing school, I expressed a wish to open a beauty parlour in Brussels. I had a great many friends in that city and I felt reasonably confident of making a success of the venture. But ... Sir Gilbert objected. At first, I couldn't quite see why he objected, and then suddenly, one morning, he told me that ... that he wanted me to be his wife. I was amazed. I'd always been fond of him, of

71

course, but I'd never, in my wildest dreams, thought of ever becoming his wife. Two weeks later, I left for Brussels.

STEVE: Please, go on …

SHEILA: While I was there, I received several letters from Sir Gilbert in which he repeated the offer he had made. I made a success of my business, and in 1938, I came to England. I was over here several weeks before I actually saw Sir Gilbert – and then he invited me to his house. Once again, he proposed, and I turned him down. But this time – this time, Mrs Temple – there was a change, a change in his attitude towards me, I mean. He'd always been so kind, so gentle, but now … he was arrogant, self-assertive, at times almost threatening. He told me quite frankly, that no matter how many times I might turn him down, he intended to have his own way. About three nights ago, I visited his house again. When I arrived, Sir Gilbert was in the study. Rather to my surprise, he was talking to a strange, rather unkempt little man he called Snooker Riley.

STEVE: (*Surprised*) Snooker Riley?

SHEILA: I overheard part of their conversation – I heard Sir Gilbert make arrangements about the revolver, the revolver that was to be placed in your bedroom and connected to the electric current. I was bewildered. I didn't know what to do. Later, during the night, I made up my mind that the best thing I could do was to telephone your husband …

STEVE: And then?

SHEILA: Last night, I saw Sir Gilbert again, and he told me that if I didn't accept his proposal of marriage, he had every intention of contacting either the police or your husband and …

72

STEVE: ... telling them that you were the leader of an organisation trafficking in drugs?

SHEILA: Yes ...

STEVE: Do you think Sir Gilbert is the leader of that organisation?

SHEILA: What organisation? I don't know, Mrs Temple ... I don't know ... I just don't know anything about that sort of thing ... (*Bewildered*) Why Sir Gilbert should suddenly take it into his head to mix with men like Snooker Riley, I don't know ... I ... really, I just don't know ...

STEVE: Is Sir Gilbert a wealthy man?

SHEILA: Well, yes, I've always thought so. He's not a millionaire, of course, but he's quite well off. (*Suddenly*) Mrs Temple, I know my story doesn't sound very plausible but, I assure you, it's the truth ...

STEVE: (*After a moment*) Thank you, Madame De Briac.

SHEILA: Please! Please! Not Madame De Briac – Sheila Baxter ... Madame De Briac is merely a professional name ...

STEVE: All right, Miss Baxter – I'll tell my husband your side of the story ...

SHEILA: Thank you, Mrs Temple! (*Pleasantly*) And now, if you really would like that permanent wave, I'll ...

A knock is heard, and the door opens.

SHEILA: Ah, come in, Charles!

KELVIN: You sent for me, Madame?

SHEILA: Yes! Charles, this is Mrs Temple. I want you to (*She breaks off; realising that they know each other*)

STEVE: (*Pleasantly*) We meet again, Mr Kelvin.

KELVIN: (*Calmly*) It would seem like it, Madame.

SHEILA: You ... know ... each other?

73

STEVE: Yes, I met Mr Kelvin …

KELVIN: I frequently had the pleasure of attending to Mrs Temple, Madame – when I was at Armand's …

SHEILA: Oh … Oh, I see …

KELVIN: This way, Madame …

FADE UP of MUSIC.

FADE DOWN of MUSIC.

A door opens.

FORBES: (*Sharply*) Yes, Peters – what is it?

PETERS: Mr Temple is here, Sir Graham.

FORBES: (*Pleasant manner*) Oh, good – ask him in, Peters!

TEMPLE enters.

TEMPLE: Hello, Sir Graham …

FORBES: Ah, come in, Temple! I've been expecting you …

TEMPLE: You look very spruce, Major! Where are you off to? Is it your night out?

PETERS: (*A sore point*) Well, officially, Mr Temple, it's supposed to be my day off, but …

FORBES: No rest for the wicked, Peters …

PETERS: Nor those who try to catch 'em either, by the look of things, sir.

TEMPLE: (*Laughing*) There's a very good detective film at the Empire, Major.

PETERS: M'm – well, if it's all the same to you, sir, I'll take Hedy Lamarr. Goodnight, sir!

FORBES and TEMPLE laugh.

FORBES: Goodnight, Peters.

PETERS: Goodnight, Temple.

TEMPLE: Goodnight, Major.

Door closes.

FORBES: Well, are you ready, Temple?

TEMPLE: Yes, I'm ready. You haven't told anyone about this little expedition, have you, Sir Graham?

FORBES: Not a soul. Sergeant Dudley's taking us out to the houseboat, but he doesn't know our destination. We'll give him his instructions once we get started.

TEMPLE: Good.

FORBES: What exactly did the letter say, Temple?

TEMPLE: It was addressed – or rather was apparently addressed to Sir Gilbert – and it said … "… Meet me, as arranged, at the houseboat. I shall be there by eleven …"

FORBES: Of course, we don't know for certain that it's Snooker Riley's houseboat …

TEMPLE: We don't know anything for certain, Sir Graham, we've just got to take a chance on it.

FORBES: Yes! Yes, I agree.

The door opens and SUPERINTENDENT WETHERBY enters.

WETHERBY: Oh, I'm sorry, sir! I've brought you the Kelvin report.

FORBES: Right – let me have it, Wetherby.

WETHERBY: Evening, Mr Temple!

TEMPLE: Good evening, Superintendent! As a matter of fact, you're just the man I want to see.

WETHERBY: Yes, sir?

TEMPLE: I want you to do a little job for me if you will? I want you to trace a car – find out who it belongs to. It's a small black car, two-seater, I'm not sure of the make … Registration number G M T 678.

WETHERBY: Certainly, Mr Temple, I'll … (*Suddenly*) GMT 678 …?

TEMPLE: That's right.

WETHERBY: Are you sure?

TEMPLE: Of course I'm sure.

WETHERBY: (*Highly amused*) Well, that won't take very long!

TEMPLE: What do you mean?

WETHERBY: (*Highy amused*) It's my car!

TEMPLE: Your car!

WETHERBY: (*Laughing*) Yes …

TEMPLE: Were you out in it last night, Superintendent?

WETHERBY: No. No, as a matter of fact, I lent it to Major Peters.

TEMPLE: Oh … Oh, I see …

WETHERBY: That's funny! That's damn funny! My car!

TEMPLE: Yes … (*Laughing*) The joke's on me, Superintendent … at least … I think it is …

FORBES: (*Briskly*) Are you ready, Temple?

TEMPLE: (*His thoughts elsewhere; pulling himself together*) M'm? Oh, yes! Oh, yes – I'm ready, Sir Graham! Goodnight, Wetherby!

WETHERBY: (*Still amused*) Goodnight, sir!

FADE UP of MUSIC.

FADE DOWN of MUSIC.

FADE UP of the sound of a police launch; background of river noises.

FORBES: You've been out here once before this week, haven't you, Temple?

TEMPLE: Yes. Wetherby and I came out two or three nights ago. It was the night that girl disappeared, Sir Graham – you remember?

FORBES: Oh, yes! Yes, Wetherby told me all about it.

SERGEANT: There's the houseboat, sir – over to starboard.

FORBES: Where? Ah, yes! Pull alongside, Sergeant – and make as little noise as possible.

SERGEANT: Very good, sir! Of course, Snooker isn't there you know, sir, they found poor old Snooker …

FORBES: (*Interrupting the SERGEANT*) Yes. Yes, we know, Sergeant.

TEMPLE: Take it quietly! Take it quietly, Sergeant!

SERGEANT: Very good, sir.

The launch pulls into the side of the houseboat.

FORBES: There doesn't appear to be anyone on board, Temple.

TEMPLE: No.

FORBES: What time do you make it?

TEMPLE: It's about ten to eleven.

FORBES: Oh, well, we're all right. We're just in nice time.

SERGEANT: What would you like me to do, sir? Would you like me to wait or cruise around for five or ten minutes?

TEMPLE: Cruise around, Sergeant, but don't keep too near the houseboat.

SERGEANT: Very good, sir.

The launch has reached the houseboat.

FORBES: Steady, Temple!

TEMPLE: I'm O.K. – just give me a hand, Sir Graham, and watch your step.

FADE DOWN of scene.

FADE UP of TEMPLE forcing a hatch on the houseboat: it finally opens.

FORBES: M'm … It's not exactly the Ritz, is it?

TEMPLE closes the hatch.

TEMPLE: It's appalling!

FORBES: Just look at the place!

TEMPLE: He must have left the cabin like this the night he … (*He stops*)

FORBES: What is it?

TEMPLE: I thought I heard something …

A pause.

FORBES: No … No, I don't think so, Temple …

TEMPLE: It looks as if Snooker existed exclusively on a diet of sardines!

FORBES: (*Laughing*) Yes … (*He lifts a sardine tin off the table*) He doesn't seem to have been very clever at opening tins either …

TEMPLE: No … (*Thoughtfully*) No, he doesn't …

FORBES: What the deuce is that supposed to be? Don't tell me that's where the poor devil slept?

TEMPLE: Yes. Although I believe in the summer, he used to … (*He stops: quietly*) Do you hear it?

A pause.

FORBES: No, I …

TEMPLE: Listen!

A motor launch is approaching the houseboat.

TEMPLE: Now do you hear it?

FORBES: Yes!

TEMPLE: Stand over there, Sir Graham – near the door …

FORBES: Now watch him, Temple!

TEMPLE: Listen!

A moment: the motor launch is very near. It stops: footsteps are heard.

FORBES: Well, whoever it is – he's on his own …

TEMPLE: Sounds like it …

Footsteps are heard on the deck …

FORBES: (*A tense whisper*) Here he comes …

TEMPLE: Sh!

The hatch is thrown open.

FORBES: (*With authority*) Don't move! Stand where you are!

PETERS: (*Astonished*) Why Sir Graham … Mr Temple …!!!

TEMPLE: Good evening, Major Peters …

FADE UP of MUSIC.

END OF EPISODE THREE

EPISODE FOUR

IN WHICH
SIR GRAHAM IS SURPRISED

OPEN TO:

ANNOUNCER: Paul Temple, the celebrated novelist and private detective, is invited by Sir Graham Forbes the Chief Commissioner of Scotland Yard and by a Major Peters who is attached to the Special Branch of the C.I.D., to discover the identity of a notorious criminal known simply as – Valentine. During the course of certain investigations, Temple makes the acquaintance of a Sir Gilbert Dryden, a Mr Charles Kelvin, and a little crook known by the name of Snooker Riley. Dryden tells Temple that he suspects that the leader of the organisation is a protégé of his, a girl called Sheila Baxter. Sheila Baxter is the proprietor of a beauty salon in the West End of London and is known professionally as Madame De Briac. One morning, at Temple's request, Mrs Temple – that is Steve – visits the beauty parlour and is informed by Sheila Baxter that …

FADE UP of SHEILA.

SHEILA: I was over here several weeks before I actually saw Sir Gilbert – and then he invited me to his house. Once again, he proposed, and I turned him down. But this time – this time, Mrs Temple – there was a change, a change in his attitude towards me, I mean. He'd always been so kind, so gentle, but now … he was arrogant, self-assertive, at times almost threatening. He told me quite frankly, that no matter how many times I might turn him down, he intended to have his own way.

83

About three nights ago, I visited his house again. When I arrived, Sir Gilbert was in the study. Rather to my surprise, he was talking to a strange, rather unkempt little man he called Snooker Riley.

STEVE: (*Surprised*) Snooker Riley?

SHEILA: I overheard part of their conversation – I heard Sir Gilbert make arrangements about the revolver, the revolver that was to be placed in your bedroom and connected to the electric current. I was bewildered. I didn't know what to do. Later, during the night, I made up my mind that the best thing I could do was to telephone your husband …

STEVE: Go on …

SHEILA: Last night, I saw Sir Gilbert again, and he told me that if I didn't accept his proposal of marriage, he had every intention of contacting either the police or your husband and …

STEVE: … telling them that you were the leader of an organisation trafficking in drugs?

SHEILA: Yes …

STEVE: Do you think Sir Gilbert is the leader of that organisation?

SHEILA: (*Puzzled*) What organisation? (*Start to FADE*) I don't know, Mrs Temple … I don't know … I just don't know anything about that sort of thing …

Complete FADE.

FADE UP of ANNOUNCER.

ANNOUNCER: Later the same day, Temple and Sir Graham Forbes pay an unexpected visit to the home of the late Mr Snooker Riley. This is a houseboat. (*Start FADE*) A somewhat dilapidated houseboat, situated on the river about two miles from Silverdale ...

FADE UP of TEMPLE forcing a hatch on the houseboat: it finally opens.

FORBES: M'm ... It's not exactly the Ritz, is it?

TEMPLE closes the hatch.

TEMPLE: It's appalling!

FORBES: Just look at the place!

TEMPLE: He must have left the cabin like this the night he ... (*He stops*)

FORBES: What is it?

TEMPLE: I thought I heard something ...

A pause.

FORBES: No ... No, I don't think so, Temple ...

TEMPLE: It looks as if Snooker existed exclusively on a diet of sardines!

FORBES: (*Laughing*) Yes ... (*He lifts a sardine tin off the table*) He doesn't seem to have been very clever at opening tins either ...

TEMPLE: No ... (*Thoughtfully*) No, he doesn't ...

FORBES: What the deuce is that supposed to be? Don't tell me that's where the poor devil slept?

TEMPLE: Yes. Although I believe in the summer, he used to ... (*He stops: quietly*) Do you hear it?

A pause.

FORBES: No, I ...

TEMPLE: Listen!

A motor launch is approaching the houseboat.

TEMPLE: Now do you hear it?

FORBES: Yes!

TEMPLE: Stand over there, Sir Graham – near the door ...

FORBES: Now watch him, Temple!

TEMPLE: Listen!

A moment: the motor launch is very near. It stops: footsteps are heard.

FORBES: Well, whoever it is – he's on his own ...

TEMPLE: Sounds like it ...

Footsteps are heard on the deck ...

FORBES: (*A tense whisper*) Here he comes ...

TEMPLE: Sh!

The hatch is thrown open.

FORBES: (*With authority*) Don't move! Stand where you are!

PETERS: (*Astonished*) Why Sir Graham ... Mr Temple ...!!!

TEMPLE: Good evening, Major Peters ...

FORBES: (*Staggered*) Peters! Peters, what on earth are you doing here?

PETERS: (*Laughing*) Well, if it comes to that, Sir Graham, what on earth are you doing here?

TEMPLE: (*Quietly, watching PETERS*) Read this letter Major Peters ...

PETERS: What is it?

TEMPLE: It was addressed to Sir Gilbert Dryden ...

PETERS: (*Reading; quickly*) ... "The package you are expecting will arrive on the 22nd. Meet me, as arranged, on the houseboat. I shall be there by eleven ... Valentine" ... Valentine! Good – Good heavens! You mean to say that you were here ... waiting for Valentine ... and I ... I turned up ...?

TEMPLE: Yes.

PETERS: But why didn't you tell me that you were coming here? Why didn't you tell me about this letter?

FORBES:	(*Faintly embarrassed*) Well …
TEMPLE:	I purposely asked Sir Graham to keep it confidential.
PETERS:	(*Not very pleased*) I see. Well, I'm afraid you've let yourself in for rather a damp squib, haven't you, Mr Temple?
TEMPLE:	(*Irritated*) What do you mean?
PETERS:	(*Laughing*) Well – you expected Valentine and …
TEMPLE:	(*Pleasantly*) We got Major Peters …
FORBES:	(*Quietly, interested*) You still haven't told us what you're doing here, Peters.
PETERS:	(*Inclined to be amused at TEMPLE and FORBES's expense*) Mr Temple isn't the only one who likes to keep things to himself! You remember that knife we found by Snooker Riley?
FORBES:	Yes.
PETERS:	It had a print on it – quite a good one.
TEMPLE:	Whose?
PETERS:	I don't know, Mr Temple – not yet. But I want to find out whether the man who handled that knife ever visited Snooker – here – on the houseboat. If he did, well – that's something to go on. You will observe, Mr Temple, that I have a fingerprint outfit with me. I hope you'll agree that that substantiates my story.
FORBES:	Your story doesn't need substantiating, Peters, if you say you came here to … (*He stops*) Listen – there's a launch!

The sound of an approaching motor launch is heard.

TEMPLE:	I think it's the Sergeant! Wait a minute!

The motor launch arrives at the houseboat.

SERGEANT:	(*Calling from outside*) Sergeant Dudley, sir!!!

TEMPLE opens the hatch.

TEMPLE: (*Calling*) We'll be with you in a moment, Sergeant!

SERGEANT: (*Calling*) Very good, sir!

FORBES: (*Through the open hatch*) Have you seen anyone?

SERGEANT: Only Major Peters, sir!

FORBES: Well – we'll leave you to it, Peters. Goodnight!

PETERS: Goodnight, Sir Graham! (*Amused*) Goodnight, Mr Temple!

TEMPLE: (*After a moment*) Goodnight, Major …

FADE UP the noise of the motor launch as it departs from the houseboat.

FADE SCENE.

FADE UP of the motor launch.

FORBES: (*Peering ahead*) Looks to me as if it's getting foggy, Temple …

TEMPLE: Doesn't look too clear … What's that place, Sergeant – over on the right?

SERGEANT: Where? Oh, that's a warehouse …

Background of river noises.

TEMPLE: You must have been up and down the river a few times, Sergeant …

SERGEANT: I wish I'd as many pounds, sir …

A pause.

FORBES: Cigarette, Temple?

TEMPLE: Thank you, Sir Graham …

FORBES: Sergeant?

SERGEANT: (*Pleased*) Oh, thank you, sir …

In the background can be heard the sound of an approaching motor launch.

TEMPLE: Hello! I wonder if this is Peters?

FORBES: Yes, it sounds like him …

TEMPLE: (*Thoughtfully*) I don't know. I should have said …

Suddenly, from the approaching motor launch, a MAN's voice can be heard calling for help. The MAN is obviously struggling with someone. He sounds both desperate and frightened.

FORBES: (*Quickly*) What's happening?

SERGEANT: It sounds to me as if …

TEMPLE: (*Quickly, tensely*) Keep well over, Sergeant, and slow down!

FORBES: I don't think it's Peters!

TEMPLE: No … No, it's certainly not his voice!

The MAN is still struggling and calling wildly for help. Suddenly, there is a revolver shot; the MAN stops struggling. He groans, and after a moment, we hear the splash as the body hits the water …

TEMPLE: (*Quickly, taking command*) Turn your light full on, Sergeant! Quickly!!!

SERGEANT: Right sir!!

FORBES: That's better!!!

SERGEANT: He's over on the …

TEMPLE: Keep her steady, Sergeant! Keep her steady!!!

FORBES: (*Tensely*) It's not Peters in the boat, Temple, although I'm damned if I can see who it is …

FORBES is interrupted by a shot. It is followed by the sudden smashing of glass.

TEMPLE: They've hit the lamp!!!

SERGEANT: There's an emergency lamp, sir, over on the …

TEMPLE: Look out!!!!

A shot is heard, and it is followed by a series of rapid repeats. It is quite obvious that a sten gun is being used.

TEMPLE: Keep down!!! Keep down, Sir Graham!!!!

The shots are repeated in rapid violent succession.

FORBES: Careful, Temple!!!!

A second spurt of machine gun fire is heard.

TEMPLE: Are … you all right, Sergeant?

SERGEANT: Yes, but I wish the swine would put his blasted light out!

Suddenly, the noise of the other boat is heard. It is departing. It quickly fades away.

FORBES: (*With relief*) He's gone …

TEMPLE: Yes …

SERGEANT: Are you O.K. sir?

FORBES: Yes … Yes, I'm O.K. Sergeant …

TEMPLE: I wonder whether the other man is, I heard him hit the water …

FORBES: Yes … You know, it sounded to me, Temple, as if the poor devil was being abducted and when he heard our launch …

TEMPLE: … decided to make a dash for it … Yes …

SERGEANT: (*Suddenly; a shout*) There he is, sir!!! Look!!!!

TEMPLE: Where? Where?! By Timothy, you're right! Pull her over, Sergeant!

The boat slows down.

FORBES: Watch yourself, Temple!

TEMPLE: Give me your hand, Sir Graham …

FORBES: For heaven's sake, don't fall overboard or we'd never …

TEMPLE: I'm all right! Give me a hand!!!! Now take it steady, Sergeant! Take … it … steady … (*Suddenly; straining*) O.K. … I've got him!!!

The water can be heard surging against the side of the boat.

FORBES: (*Straining; holding TEMPLE back*) Try … and … get hold of his arms, Temple … if you can …

TEMPLE: Pull … Pull, Sir Graham … (*Breathlessly*) Here he comes!

With a tremendous effort, TEMPLE and FORBES manage to extricate the MAN from the water. They stand for a moment breathing heavily – trying to regain their breath.

FORBES: He's not an Englishman … Looks to me like a Chinese …

SERGEANT: Whatever he is, sir – he looks a goner!

FORBES: Yes … Yes, I'm afraid you're right, Sergeant …

TEMPLE: They've shot him!

FORBES: Yes … Do – do you recognise him, Temple?

TEMPLE: (*Thoughtfully*) No … No, I've never seen him before … I wonder who he is …?

SERGEANT: Shall I search him, sir, or …

TEMPLE: (*Suddenly*) Wait a minute, Sergeant … He's got something in his hand, it looks to me like … a watch chain … Yes … Yes, it is …

SERGEANT: He must have pulled it off the man he was struggling with, sir – the man on the boat.

TEMPLE: (*Interested*) Yes …

FORBES: (*Quietly, extremely interested*) Temple – Temple, I've seen that watch chain somewhere before …

TEMPLE: You certainly have, Sir Graham – and I know where!!!!

FORBES: Where?

TEMPLE: On Mr Charles Kelvin …

FADE UP of MUSIC.

FADE DOWN of MUSIC.
FADE UP of SIR GRAHAM.

FORBES: … Well, I'm glad you've taken me into your confidence, Temple. But it seems to me that we've got to believe one or the other – we can't believe both. Either Miss Baxter is lying about

91

Sir Gilbert, or Sir Gilbert is lying about Miss Baxter. Now, in view of what you've told me …

TEMPLE: Yes?

FORBES: I put my money on the girl. I think she's telling the truth.

TEMPLE: So does Steve – but I'm not sure.

FORBES: Well, Miss Baxter – or Madame De Briac if you like – has got a pretty flourishing business, Temple. She's a good-looking girl too, just the sort of girl Sir Gilbert would fall for.

TEMPLE: Does … he … fall easily for the …?

FORBES: According to all accounts easily and frequently!

TEMPLE: M'm – I see. Of course, even if she is telling the truth, it doesn't necessarily mean that Sir Gilbert is Valentine. Just as, if …

FORBES: If he's telling the truth, it doesn't necessarily mean that she's Valentine either.

TEMPLE: Exactly.

FORBES: Have you seen this girl – Sheila Baxter – yourself?

TEMPLE: No. I'm seeing her tonight. Steve's invited her to the flat.

FORBES: Good. I think that's …

A knock and the door opens.

FORBES: What is it, Wetherby?

WETHERBY: I'm sorry to interrupt, sir – but Kelvin's here.

FORBES: Oh. All right, Wetherby – ask him in. (*Suddenly*) Oh – did you mention the watch chain?

WETHERBY: Not a word, sir.

FORBES: Good.

TEMPLE: Oh, Superintendent …

92

WETHERBY: Yes, Mr Temple …?

TEMPLE: Is Major Peters in?

WETHERBY: Yes, I believe he's in his office, sir.

TEMPLE: Well, would you be kind enough to give him this cigarette case – handle it carefully. Tell him, I believe there's a fingerprint on it and I'd like him to check it with the one we found on the knife – the knife that killed Snooker Riley.

WETHERBY: Very good, sir. (*Interested: pleasantly*) Oh, er – whose print is it, Mr Temple?

TEMPLE: (*Pleasantly; laughing it off*) We'll discuss that later, Superintendent.

WETHERBY: Very good, sir.

The door closes.

TEMPLE: You sent for Kelvin?

FORBES: Yes. I thought we might as well hear what he's got to say. By the way, I had a report through this morning from the League of Nations people – they check-up for us, you know, on the distribution of narcotics. The figures have risen during the past two or three months, I'm afraid.

TEMPLE: M'm …

FORBES: You know, Temple, the thing that beats me is where exactly Valentine makes his contacts. He must have a sort of distribution centre, almost … a kind of … headquarters …

TEMPLE: Did you check on The Simon Lee?

FORBES: Yes. We checked on The Simon Lee all right, but it seems a pretty reliable sort of vessel; belongs to a first-class company. Of course, O'Hara – the real Captain O'Hara – was mixed up in this business, but so far as we can make out, the rest of the crew seem to be pretty straight.

TEMPLE: M'm. I'd like to get my hands on the man who impersonated O'Hara …

FORBES: If we once get that bird in the cage and made him talk, we'd be getting somewhere!

TEMPLE: (*Grimly*) I'd make him talk all right …

The door opens.

WETHERBY: Mr Kelvin, sir.

FORBES: Thank you, Wetherby. Come in, Kelvin!

The door closes.

FORBES: Sit down …

KELVIN: Good morning, Mr Temple …

TEMPLE: Good morning …

FORBES: (*Briskly*) Sit down, Kelvin! Sit down!

KELVIN: Superintendent Wetherby told me that you wanted to see me Sir Graham and …

FORBES: Yes, I want you to have a look at this …

A drawer is opened.

KELVIN: (*Nervously*) What is it? It's a watch-chain of course, but …

FORBES: Don't you recognise it?

KELVIN: Why, no!

FORBES: Isn't it yours?

KELVIN: (*A nervous laugh*) I've never seen it in my life before …

TEMPLE: Haven't you, Mr Kelvin? (*Forcefully*) Haven't you …?

KELVIN: (*Hesitant*) Well – as a matter of fact it is mine only …

FORBES: (*Sharply*) Only what?

KELVIN: Where did you find it?

TEMPLE: Where would you expect us to find it, Mr Kelvin?

KELVIN: I don't know, sir. I – I lost the chain two or three days ago. I – I think I lost it the day my wife died.

FORBES: I see. Mr Kevin, tell me: is Charlie King a friend of yours?

KELVIN: Charlie King?

FORBES: Yes.

KELVIN: I've never heard of the gentleman. What makes you think that he might be a friend of mine?

TEMPLE: (*Slowly; watching KELVIN*) We picked him out of the river last night – he had your watch chain.

KELVIN: (*Thoughtfully; apparently sincere*) Charlie King ...? No ... No ... I've never heard of anyone called Charlie King ...

TEMPLE: (*Lightly; a change of manner*) Mr Kelvin, my wife tells me that you work for Madame De Briac?

KELVIN: Yes. Yes, Mr Temple ...

TEMPLE: How long have you been there?

KELVIN: Just a fortnight.

TEMPLE: When my wife said that you'd met before, I believe you deliberately ...

KELVIN: (*Interrupting TEMPLE*) I told Madame De Briac that I'd ... attended to Mrs Temple ... at my last place, but ... that was not true.

TEMPLE: (*Quite simply*) Then why did you say it?

KELVIN: (*Hesitant; uncertain of himself*) Because I didn't want Madame De Briac to know that I'd met Mrs Temple with Superintendent Wetherby ...

TEMPLE: Oh?

FORBES: Why not?

95

KELVIN:	Well – it's difficult to explain … but … you see … when my wife committed suicide, I received an awful lot of publicity. Madame De Briac was nice about things, of course, but … well … you know … publicity of that kind is not good for business … not for a business like Madame De Briac's …
FORBES:	(*Not believing a word*) I see …

The door opens.

WETHERBY:	Excuse me, sir – but Bradley's just sent this report through on Charlie King. I thought you might like to see it. (*Significantly*) It's interesting, sir.
FORBES:	Yes. Yes, all right! Mr Kelvin, would you mind stepping into the other office for a moment? Show Mr Kelvin into Inspector White's office, will you, Wetherby?
WETHERBY:	Very good, sir.

The door closes.

FORBES:	(*Quietly; confidentially*) That boy's not telling the truth.
TEMPLE:	No.
FORBES:	Shall we pick him up?
TEMPLE:	(*Thoughtfully*) No. No, I don't think so, Sir Graham – not … just … at the moment.
FORBES:	Do you think …
TEMPLE:	What?
FORBES:	Do you think he's Valentine?
TEMPLE:	Do you, Sir Graham?
FORBES:	(*Worried*) I don't know. I don't know, Temple.

The door opens. Wetherby returns.

WETHERBY:	It's an interesting report on Charlie King, sir.
FORBES:	Well, let's have it, Wetherby.

WETHERBY: He was 47. Lived in Charters Street. Was single but apparently lived with an Italian girl. He did a stretch in Sing-Sing in 1926 for peddling dope and ...

FORBES: That's interesting.

WETHERBY: And another stretch in '31. In 1938 he bought the San Chow restaurant in Eden Street and ...

TEMPLE: (*Surprised*) The San Chow restaurant? That's quite an expensive sort of place.

TEMPLE is interrupted by the door: MAJOR PETERS has entered.

PETERS: (*Quite excited*) Mr Temple!

FORBES: What is it, Peters?

TEMPLE: Yes, Major?

PETERS: (*Quite excited*) Mr Temple, that cigarette case ... the one you sent down with Superintendent Wetherby ... I've compared the fingerprint with the one on the knife ... the knife that killed Snooker Riley ...

TEMPLE: (*Interested*) Well?

PETERS: (*A moment*) They're identical!

TEMPLE: (*Quietly*) You're positive?

PETERS: Absolutely positive!

FORBES: (*Quickly*) Whose is it? Whose fingerprint is it, Temple?

TEMPLE: (*Completely ignoring the question; thoughtfully*) Now that's interesting ... interesting ...

FADE UP of MUSIC.

FADE DOWN of MUSIC.
FADE UP of STEVE.

STEVE: ... Won't you have another drink, Miss Baxter?

97

SHEILA: No. No, really. I must be going. I've got an appointment at …

TEMPLE: (*Mixing a drink*) Nonsense! Of course you mustn't be going! Here we are, Steve! Give this to Miss Baxter …

SHEILA: No, really, Mr Temple, I … I … I … (*Laughs*) Thanks!

TEMPLE: Skoal!

SHEILA: (*After drinking*) Brrr!

STEVE: Darling, you always mix them too strong!

SHEILA: (*Laughing*) It's dynamite!

TEMPLE: (*After a little laugh*) I'm awfully grateful to you for coming along here tonight and telling me your story.

SHEILA: I'm afraid it doesn't sound a very plausible one, Mr Temple, whichever way one looks at it.

TEMPLE: Miss Baxter, I meant to ask you – how long have you known Mr Kelvin?

SHEILA: Mr Kelvin? Oh, Charles! About two months – he used to work for Armand before … (*A sudden thought*) Mr Temple, you don't think that Charles Kelvin's mixed up in this business, do you?

TEMPLE: Well – his wife committed suicide, you know that, don't you?

SHEILA: Yes. Yes, I know, but … (*Thoughtfully*) She was a strange, emotional sort of girl … Did you ever meet her?

TEMPLE: No.

SHEILA: She came to the shop once or twice to see Charles … I rather liked her but she always seemed so highly strung – so sensitive … I do hope Charles isn't mixed up in this affair, Mr Temple, because publicity – the wrong sort of publicity – isn't good for my type of business you know …

TEMPLE: No, I suppose it isn't.

SHEILA: (*Suddenly*) Well, now I must be going!

TEMPLE: Have another drink!

SHEILA: (*Emphatically*) No! NO!!!

STEVE: It's a pity you can't stay and have dinner with us.

TEMPLE: As a matter of fact, we're going out, darling – but why don't you join us?

SHEILA: That's awfully sweet of you both, but I've got a date!

TEMPLE: Well, some other time. We'll make a night of it.

SHEILA: I'd like to.

STEVE: Where are we going, Paul?

TEMPLE: I've booked a table at the San Chow, darling – for eight o'clock.

STEVE: The San Chow?

TEMPLE: Yes, it's in Eden Street. Remember, Steve, we went there once before …

SHEILA: It's a Chinese restaurant, isn't it?

TEMPLE: Yes.

STEVE: Oh, I remember!

SHEILA: Goodnight, Mr Temple!

TEMPLE: Goodnight, Miss Baxter!

The door opens and closes.

TEMPLE whistles to himself; mixes another drink.

The door opens and STEVE returns.

STEVE: Well?

TEMPLE: Well, what, darling?

STEVE: What do you think of Madame De Briac?

TEMPLE: Oh, she's more or less what you described.

STEVE: Did you believe her story?

TEMPLE: It was … interesting. Do you want another drink?

STEVE: No. No, I suppose I'd better get changed.

TEMPLE: (*A moment*) You remember that knife, Steve – the one that killed Snooker Riley?

STEVE: Yes.

TEMPLE: Major Peters found a fingerprint on it. It was Sir Gilbert Dryden's.

STEVE: (*Surprised*) Sir Gilbert Dryden's!

TEMPLE: Yes.

STEVE: Well, doesn't that more or less confirm what Miss Baxter told us. She said she overheard Sir Gilbert talking to Snooker Riley about the revolver. The one in our bedroom. The one that …

Suddenly, from downstairs, a quick piercing scream can be heard. SHEILA BAXTER is screaming and struggling; she is frightened.

STEVE: What's that?

TEMPLE: (*Quickly; tensely*) It's Miss Baxter! Wait here, Steve!

TEMPLE crosses the room, and the door is thrown open.
FADE SCENE.

Quick FADE UP of SHEILA BAXTER. She is no longer screaming or struggling, but she is gasping for breath and obviously sounds as if she is suffering from shock and the after-effects of a violent struggle.

TEMPLE: (*Arriving; breathless*) Miss Baxter! What is it? Are you all right?

SHEILA: Yes … Yes … Yes, I'm all right … but … (*She is frightened, near hysteria*) … My throat, it's …

TEMPLE: (*Gently*) Now take it easy, Miss Baxter … Take it easy … You're all right …

SHEILA: I – I was getting out of the lift when someone came up behind me, he must have come up the stairs from the basement because … Oh, it was horrible! Horrible!!!

TEMPLE: (*Softly*) Now just take it easy, Miss Baxter – there's nothing to worry about.

SHEILA: I – I felt his hands on my neck … I felt his hands
         getting tighter and tighter. I felt his hands … Oh, it
         was horrible!!!!

STEVE arrives.

STEVE: (*Breathlessly*) Are you all right, Miss Baxter?

TEMPLE: Yes, she's all right, darling! (*Quickly*) Did you
         recognise him?

SHEILA: No. No, I was so frightened I didn't even look at
         his face … I caught hold of his jacket; I screamed, I
         scratched, I kicked, I … (*For the first time seeing
         the humorous side of the situation*) I don't know
         what I didn't do!

STEVE: Well, you succeeded in tearing a button off his
         jacket …

TEMPLE: Where?

STEVE: Look! It's on the floor.

TEMPLE: Well, that ought to be useful … Where's your car,
         Miss Baxter?

SHEILA: It's just round the corner.

TEMPLE: Do you feel well enough to drive?

SHEILA: Yes … Yes … I – I feel much better now … thanks
         … (*Worried, almost frightened again*) I wonder who
         it was. Mr Temple?

TEMPLE: (*Gently*) Just don't think about it … Come along …
         Come along to the car!

FADE UP of MUSIC.

*FADE DOWN and CROSS FADE to music at the San Chow
restaurant.*

*FADE DOWN of MUSIC to distant background; it is a quiet
restaurant with a definite atmosphere: the restaurant orchestra
stops.*

WAITER: Would you like some more coffee, madam?

STEVE: No, I don't think so. You know, I don't remember coming to this restaurant after all, Paul!

TEMPLE: Don't you? It's not so long ago. Ricky told us about it.

STEVE: Oh, yes. Yes, of course! (*Laughs*) I wonder how he's getting on.

TEMPLE: Ricky? He's getting on all right – you leave that to Ricky.

STEVE: Why you wanted to introduce him to that film director heaven only knows! We lost the best servant we ever had.

TEMPLE: (*After a laugh*) There's one thing about this place – you can be nice and confidential. I rather like all this partition nonsense!

STEVE: I suspect we're the only married couple in the place.

TEMPLE: That's just what I was thinking.

STEVE: You say this place belonged to Charlie King, the man you picked out of the river last night … (*She stops, noticing TEMPLE's expression*) What is it, Paul?

TEMPLE: (*Softly*) Look who's here!

STEVE: (*Quietly, suspicious*) Sir Gilbert Dryden! Now I wonder why on earth he …

TEMPLE: Sh!

SIR GILBERT arrives at the table.

DRYDEN:(*Pleasant; but a little nervous*) Hello, Mr Temple – so we meet again, sir. Good evening, Mrs Temple.

STEVE: Good evening.

TEMPLE: I didn't expect to see you here, Sir Gilbert …

DRYDEN:(*A little surprised*) No? I quite frequently dine here, Mr Temple. I suppose you might almost call me an habitué. (*Suddenly, nervously*) Mr Temple, forgive my asking, but …

TEMPLE: Yes?

DRYDEN: Did you visit the houseboat last night? Remember you …

TEMPLE: (*Quietly*) Yes, we visited the houseboat, Sir Gilbert.

DRYDEN: (*Quickly*) What happened?

TEMPLE: Oh … Oh, nothing of importance …

DRYDEN: Valentine didn't … turn … up … then?

TEMPLE: Not unless Valentine happens to be Sir Graham Forbes.

DRYDEN laughs.

TEMPLE: Or Major Peters.

DRYDEN: Major Peters?

TEMPLE: Major Peters is attached to the Special Branch.

DRYDEN: Oh. (*Almost relieved*) Oh, I see. (*Suddenly*) Ah, I see my friend has arrived! Please excuse me. Goodbye, Mrs Temple.

STEVE: Goodbye, Sir Gilbert.

DRYDEN: Goodbye, Temple.

TEMPLE: Goodnight, Sir Gilbert.

A moment.

STEVE: (*Quickly; excitedly*) Darling! Darling, did you see his coat! The button! The bottom button of his jacket …

TEMPLE: (*Quietly*) It was missing … Yes, Steve, I noticed it.

STEVE: (*Excitedly*) Paul! Paul, that proves conclusively that …

TEMPLE: It doesn't prove anything, darling! It only … (*Suddenly, quietly astonished*) By Timothy! By Timothy, Steve!

STEVE: (*Quickly, almost alarmed*) What is it?

TEMPLE: (*Tensely*) That man … the man Sir Gilbert's talking to …

STEVE: Well?

103

TEMPLE: (*Seriously*) That's the gentleman I've been looking for …

STEVE: Who is it?

TEMPLE: (*Slowly*) It's the man that impersonated O'Hara!

STEVE: (*Astonished*) Are you sure?

TEMPLE: (*Quickly; having made a sudden decision*) Yes … Yes … Now listen! Listen, Steve! I want you to go outside and get the car … Meet me at the front entrance and keep the engine running …

STEVE: But …

TEMPLE: Now darling, please, do as I tell you …

STEVE: (*Tensely*) Yes … Yes, all right …

The restaurant orchestra starts to play again.

TEMPLE: Oh! Chan!

WAITER: Sir?

TEMPLE: (*Casually*) Who's that gentleman talking to Sir Gilbert Dryden?

WAITER: Where, sir? Oh! Oh, that's an American gentleman, sir. A Mr Layland.

TEMPLE: Well, would you be good enough to tell Mr Layland I'd like to see him in the … in the entrance hall …

WAITER: Certainly, sir. Your name?

TEMPLE: (*Hesitating a moment*) Er … tell him … Mr Kelvin would like to see him … Mr … Charles Kelvin.

WAITER: (*A little puzzled*) Yes, sir …

TEMPLE: Here you are …

WAITER: (*Much brighter*) Oh, thank you, sir … Mr Kelvin you said, sir?

TEMPLE: That's right … Mr Kelvin … Oh, and waiter – if you can possibly help it, don't let Sir Gilbert hear what you're saying.

WAITER: Very good, sir.

FADE UP of restaurant orchestra.

Slow FADE DOWN to the background.

TEMPLE: (*Quietly*) Are you looking for someone, Mr Layland?

LAYLAND: (*An American: but not too broad*) Yeah, the waiter said that … (*He recognises TEMPLE*) … that …

TEMPLE: (*Slowly*) Remember me? It's a small world, isn't it … Captain O'Hara …?

LAYLAND: What do you mean? Is this some kind of gag because if it is I … (*He stops: nervously*) What – what's that you've got … in … your pocket …?

TEMPLE: (*Politely*) What does it look like, Mr Layland?

LAYLAND: It – it looks like a revolver …

TEMPLE: And that's precisely what it is …

A pause.

LAYLAND: What do you want me to do?

TEMPLE: I want you to turn round … walk straight out of here … and get in my car …

LAYLAND: And just supposing …

TEMPLE: Yes?

LAYLAND: (*Almost a threat*) Just supposing I don't walk straight out of here, Mr Temple?

TEMPLE: (*Quite pleasantly*) Then you'll be carried out, Mr Layland – on a stretcher …

FADE UP of MUSIC.

END OF EPISODE FOUR

EPISODE FIVE

IN WHICH MR LAYLAND
TELLS THE TRUTH

ANNOUNCER: Paul Temple, the celebrated novelist and private detective, is invited by Sir Graham Forbes, the Chief Commissioner of Scotland Yard, to investigate the activities of a drug smuggling organisation under the leadership of a notorious criminal known simply as Valentine. During the course of investigations, Temple makes the acquaintance of a Sir Gilbert Dryden, and a Mr Charles Kelvin. Dryden tells Temple that he suspects that the leader of the organisation – Valentine – is a protegé of his, a girl called Sheila Baxter. Sheila Baxter is the proprietor of a beauty salon in the West End of London and is known professionally as Madame De Briac. One night, Temple together with Steve, his wife, visits the San Chow – a Chinese restaurant in Eden Street. To their surprise, Sir Gilbert Dryden is at the restaurant, and he is dining with a man for whom both Scotland Yard and Paul Temple have been searching. It is the man that impersonated a certain Captain O'Hara …

FADE UP of MUSIC.

Quick FADE DOWN of MUSIC.

TEMPLE: (*Tensely*) That man … the man Sir Gilbert's talking to …

STEVE: Well?

TEMPLE: (*Seriously*) That's the gentleman I've been looking for …

STEVE: Who is it?

TEMPLE: (*Slowly*) It's the man that impersonated O'Hara!

STEVE:	(*Astonished*) Are you sure?
TEMPLE:	(*Quickly; having made a sudden decision*) Yes … Yes … Now listen! Listen, Steve! I want you to go outside and get the car … Meet me at the front entrance and keep the engine running …
STEVE:	But …
TEMPLE:	Now darling, please, do as I tell you …
STEVE:	(*Tensely*) Yes … Yes, all right …

The restaurant orchestra starts to play again.

TEMPLE:	Oh! Chan!
WAITER:	Sir?
TEMPLE:	(*Casually*) Who's that gentleman talking to Sir Gilbert Dryden?
WAITER:	Where, sir? Oh! Oh, that's an American gentleman, sir. A Mr Layland.
TEMPLE:	Well, would you be good enough to tell Mr Layland I'd like to see him in the … in the entrance hall …
WAITER:	Certainly, sir. Your name?
TEMPLE:	(*Hesitating a moment*) Er … tell him … Mr Kelvin would like to see him … Mr … Charles Kelvin.
WAITER:	(*A little puzzled*) Yes, sir …
TEMPLE:	Here you are …
WAITER:	(*Much brighter*) Oh, thank you, sir … Mr Kelvin you said, sir?
TEMPLE:	That's right … Mr Kelvin … Oh, and waiter – if you can possibly help it, don't let Sir Gilbert hear what you're saying.
WAITER:	Very good, sir.

FADE UP of restaurant orchestra.

Slow FADE DOWN to the background.

TEMPLE: (*Quietly*) Are you looking for someone, Mr Layland?

LAYLAND: (*An American: but not too broad*) Yeah, the waiter said that ... (*He recognises TEMPLE*) ... that ...

TEMPLE: (*Slowly*) Remember me? It's a small world, isn't it ... Captain O'Hara ...?

LAYLAND: What do you mean? Is this some kind of gag because if it is I ... (*He stops: nervously*) What – what's that you've got ... in ... your pocket ...?

TEMPLE: (*Politely*) What does it look like, Mr Layland?

LAYLAND: It – it looks like a revolver ...

TEMPLE: And that's precisely what it is ...

A pause.

LAYLAND: What do you want me to do?

TEMPLE: I want you to turn round ... walk straight out of here ... and get in my car ...

LAYLAND: And just supposing ...

TEMPLE: Yes?

LAYLAND: (*Almost a threat*) Just supposing I don't walk straight out of here, Mr Temple?

TEMPLE: (*Quite pleasantly*) Then you'll be carried out, Mr Layland – on a stretcher ...

FADE UP of MUSIC.

FADE DOWN of MUSIC.
A flat buzzer is heard. The door quickly opens.

MARY: I'm sorry to keep ye waiting, ma'am, but ... (*She notices the revolver in TEMPLE's pocket*) Good gracious me, Mr Temple, is that a revolver ye ...

STEVE: That's all right, Mary. Just – just go back to the kitchen for a moment.

111

MARY: (*Seriously*) Yes … Yes, Mrs Temple.

TEMPLE: Go through to the lounge, Mr Layland – it's on your left.

The door closes.

LAYLAND: M'm. A nice place you've got here.

TEMPLE: We like it.

A door opens; Temple, STEVE and LAYLAND enter the lounge.

LAYLAND: Very nice! And they say crime doesn't pay!

TEMPLE: (*Pleasantly*) Ah, but I only write about it, Mr Layland!

LAYLAND: Yeah. You know, I've got a hunch that isn't a revolver in your pocket after all, Mr Temple.

TEMPLE: Have you? (*He takes the revolver out of his pocket*) Well, I'm sorry to disappoint you.

LAYLAND: Oh …

TEMPLE: Would you like me to prove to you that it's loaded?

LAYLAND: No … No … I'll take your word for it.

TEMPLE: Good. Sit down, Mr Layland – take the armchair.

LAYLAND: I'm O.K. Do you mind if I ask you why exactly you brought me back here?

TEMPLE: I brought you back here, Mr Layland, because I want to have a little chat with you.

LAYLAND: (*Laughing; but watching him*) A little chat? Is that so? Mr Temple, tell me, just to what extent do you think I'm mixed up in this business?

TEMPLE: Supposing you tell me, Mr Layland?

LAYLAND: Well, now, supposing I do – will you believe me?

TEMPLE: We shall see, Mr Layland – we shall see.

LAYLAND: O.K. I'll tell you – so far as I am concerned – exactly how the whole business started. Two days ago – about half past seven in the morning

112

- I was sitting in my flat with a first-class hangover and a jug of black coffee when suddenly, to my surprise (*Start FADE-BACK MUSIC*) I heard the doorbell ringing ...

Quick FADE UP of MUSIC.

MUSIC FADES.
Sound of the door bell. The door is opened.

LAYLAND: Take it easy! Take it easy, brother!

KELVIN: Mr Layland?

LAYLAND: Yeah.

KELVIN: My name is Kelvin. Charles Kelvin. May I ... come ... in, Mr Layland?

LAYLAND: (*A moment; a shrug*) What can I lose?

Door closes.

KELVIN: (*Pleasantly; but a little nervous*) Your name has been suggested to me by an old friend of yours, Mr Layland. A certain Mr Snipey Jackson.

LAYLAND: (*Surprised*) Snipey Jackson? Don't tell me they've let that guy out again!

KELVIN: (*Amused*) May I sit down?

LAYLAND: Sure! Sure! Make yourself at home. You wouldn't like a first-class hangover ...?

KELVIN: Not just at the moment, Mr Layland ...

LAYLAND: Well – what can I do for you?

KELVIN: (*Rather pleased with the way things are going*) How would you like to earn two hundred pounds, Mr Layland – in a quarter of an hour ...?

LAYLAND: (*A moment; quietly*) O.K. Let's have it!

KELVIN: Your friend, Mr Jackson, informs me that you are able to impersonate people, to – what shall we say? – pass yourself off as an entirely different personality.

113

LAYLAND: My friend, Mr Jackson, talks too much … However, go on …

KELVIN: Tonight, Mr Layland, I would like you to visit a public house in Limehouse called The Marquis of Bude and introduce yourself to a certain Mr Paul Temple as Captain O'Hara. Captain Michael Shaun Dougherty O'Hara, skipper of The Simon Lee.

LAYLAND: Go on …

KELVIN: Mr Temple will ask you a number of questions. He will ask you, for instance, what exactly you know about a person called Valentine. In answer to that question, you will tell him a story. A rather interesting – but purely fictitious – story about a certain Sir Gilbert Dryden; about a woman in Amsterdam; about a mysterious parcel; and about an address in Estonia Avenue.

LAYLAND: In other words, I meet this guy Temple, introduce myself as Captain O'Hara, and tell him – exactly – what – you – want – me – to – tell – him …

KELVIN: That's right, Mr Layland …

LAYLAND: What's he like to look at – O'Hara, I mean?

KELVIN: Don't worry about your appearance; Temple has never met O'Hara. Just be Irish – excitable – you know the type.

LAYLAND: (*In his O'HARA manner*) Ah, to be sure I know the type backwards! If it's Captain O'Hara ye be wanting ye can have the gentleman.

KELVIN: (*Amused*) Excellent, Mr Layland! Excellent!

LAYLAND: Well, if it's that good, brother, it'll cost you two hundred and fifty!

Quick FADE UP of MUSIC.

Quick FADE DOWN of MUSIC.
FADE UP of LAYLAND.

LAYLAND: … Well, there you are, that's the whole story. I turned up at The Marquis of Bude and dished out the Captain O'Hara act. And boy, I bet you fell for it.

TEMPLE: Indeed, yes, Mr Layland. In fact, my wife and I went so far as to visit four hundred and seventy-nine Estonia Avenue …

LAYLAND: (*Laughing*) No kiddin'?

TEMPLE: (*A note of authority creeping into his voice*) And do you know what we found at four hundred and seventy-nine Estonia Avenue, Mr Layland?

LAYLAND: (*No longer amused*) No …?

TEMPLE: We found the dead body of the REAL Captain O'Hara!

LAYLAND: (*Shocked*) What! I – I don't believe it! You're kiddin' …

TEMPLE: (*Quietly*) What was this man – Charles Kelvin – like?

LAYLAND: He was about twenty-eight or nine. Dark. Good-looking sort of guy, I guess. He spoke with an accent.

TEMPLE: (*To himself*) Yes. Yes, that's Kelvin …

LAYLAND: (*Nervously*) Mr Temple, was that on the level about the real Captain O'Hara?

TEMPLE: Yes.

LAYLAND: What happened to him?

TEMPLE: (*Quietly; watching LAYLAND*) Don't you know?

LAYLAND: (*Quickly*) No! No, I swear I don't …

TEMPLE: He was murdered …

LAYLAND: Murdered? (*Genuinely nervous*) Gee …
           (*Quickly*) Now don't get me wrong! I'm no
           soft-hearted lily! Play a guy for a sucker, that's
           O.K.! That's fine! But murder – murder! –
           that's a different kettle of fish.

TEMPLE: Mr Layland, tell me: why did you meet Sir
           Gilbert Dryden tonight at the San Chow?

LAYLAND: Well, that's the other side of the story. Mr
           Temple, you see … (*Hesitates*) Say, but just a
           minute! When that waiter spoke to me in the
           restaurant he said: "There's a Mr Kelvin would
           like to see you, sir – in the entrance hall."

TEMPLE: That's right. I told him to say that.

LAYLAND: You did?!

TEMPLE: Yes. You see, Mr Layland, I knew that if I said
           the name Temple you wouldn't want to see me,
           and secondly …

LAYLAND: Yes?

TEMPLE: Secondly, I just wondered if by any chance the
           name Charles Kelvin meant anything to you.

LAYLAND: Well, it did, and now you know why … it …
           did …

TEMPLE: Yes.

LAYLAND: I take it that you'd heard of Kelvin before I …

TEMPLE: Yes … I'd heard of Mr Kelvin.

LAYLAND: (*Suddenly; making up his mind*) O.K. Now I'll
           tell you the rest of my story – in other words,
           why I met Sir Gilbert tonight. The first I met
           this guy Sir Gilbert, was exactly twenty-four
           hours ago.

TEMPLE: (*Rather surprised*) Last night?

LAYLAND: Yeah. I popped into the San Chow for a bit to
           eat at about – oh, about a quarter after seven, I
           guess …

116

TEMPLE:	Alone?
LAYLAND:	No. I had a dame with me. Maisie Bell! What a name and what a gel! Boy, could she talk! She started at five minutes after seven and at ten minutes to eight she hadn't even changed gear!

...

Quick FADE UP of MUSIC.

FADE DOWN of MUSIC.
FADE UP of MAISIE BELL.

MAISIE:	... So, I said to Alice, I said: "Crikey, Alice, it's the first dress I've had in six months, you can hardly expect a ..." Here! (*Suspiciously*) Are you listening?
LAYLAND:	(*Quickly; eating his dinner; hasn't heard a word*) Sure ... sure ...
MAISIE:	(*Satisfied*) "You can hardly expect a girl in my position," I said, "to go about in rags. Why, good gracious me, Alice," I said, "it isn't as if I had alimony pouring in on me from the four corners of the earth, and then ..."
WAITER:	(*Interrupting MAISIE*) Excuse me, sir.
LAYLAND:	Oh, what is it?
WAITER:	The gentleman in the corner says that he would appreciate it if you could spare him a few moments, sir.
LAYLAND:	(*Surprised*) Where? Which gentleman?
WAITER:	In the corner, sir.
LATLAND:	Oh. Who is he, do you know?
WAITER:	It's Sir Gilbert Dryden, sir.
LAYLAND:	Oh. O.K.! O.K., tell him I'll be right over!
MAISIE:	(*Quickly*) Just a minute! No funny business!
LAYLAND:	What do you mean?
MAISIE:	I don't want to be stuck with the check.

117

LAYLAND: Don't be crazy! O.K., waiter …
FADE across room.

FADE UP.
LAYLAND: (*Not too pleasant*) I got your message. What's
            it all about?
DRYDEN: (*Pleasantly*) Mr Layland?
LAYLAND: (*Surprised*) Yeah …
DRYDEN: My name is Dryden – Sir Gilbert Dryden.
            Won't you sit down, Mr Layland?
LAYLAND: (*A moment; suspiciously*) Thanks …
DRYDEN: I'm sorry if I interrupted a tete-a-tete …
            (*Suddenly*) Would you care for a cigar?
LAYLAND: Well … thanks …
A moment; DRYDEN lights the cigar for LAYLAND.
DRYDEN: I called at your flat, Mr Layland, but the porter
            said that you were out. This is rather a lucky
            coincidence.
LAYLAND: (*Still suspicious*) Yeah …
DRYDEN: (*Slightly amused*) I can see that you don't
            entirely trust me, Mr Layland.
LAYLAND: Shall we get to the point?
DRYDEN: I'm told that for a certain consideration you do
            a very remarkable impersonation of a certain
            Captain O'Hara.
LAYLAND: Who told you that?
DRYDEN: (*A moment*) Mr Kelvin.
LAYLAND: Go on …
DRYDEN: I – I would like to put a proposition to you, Mr
            Layland, but I find myself in rather a difficult
            position.
LAYLAND: What is the proposition?
DRYDEN: Well …

118

LAYLAND: Listen! You can set your mind at rest, brother!
             If the proposition doesn't interest me, I shall
             forget it …

DRYDEN: (*Faintly amused*) I – er – I see you get the
             point. Well, briefly, Mr Layland, the
             proposition is this. In the early hours of
             Saturday morning – that's the day after
             tomorrow – an aeroplane will arrive from the
             Continent. It will land at a quiet, secluded spot
             near … near a certain village in Sussex. The
             pilot of the aeroplane will have a package – a
             large, and rather important package, Mr
             Layland. He has agreed to hand that package
             over to … to … Captain O'Hara.

LAYLAND: And you want me … to … be … Captain
             O'Hara?

DRYDEN: If you please, Mr Layland.

LAYLAND: Has this guy – the aeroplane guy – ever seen
             the real Captain O'Hara?

DRYDEN: (*After a momentary hesitation*) Once – a long
             time ago. But that shouldn't present any
             difficulties – it will be quite dark when the
             plane arrives. So far as you are concerned, it
             will simply mean a brief conversation with the
             pilot and the handing over of the package.

LAYLAND: And then what do I do – bring the package
             back to London?

DRYDEN: No. You'll – er – simply deliver it to an address
             in the village.

LAYLAND: I see. But tell me, why can't the real Captain
             O'Hara …

DRYDEN: (*Interrupting*) The real Captain O'Hara is
             regrettably indisposed.

A slight pause.

119

LAYLAND: O.K. How much?

DRYDEN: What did Mr Kelvin pay you?

LAYLAND: (*Without a moment's hesitation*) Three fifty …

DRYDEN: (*Slightly amused*) He paid you two fifty, Mr Layland – however – on this occasion, as you say, it should be three fifty …

A moment.

LAYLAND: O.K. It's a deal.

DRYDEN: Then meet me here tomorrow night and I'll give you your instructions …

LAYLAND: At eight o'clock?

DRYDEN: At eight o'clock, Mr Layland.

Quick FADE UP of MUSIC.

FADE DOWN of MUSIC.

FADE UP of LAYLAND.

LAYLAND: … and that's the truth, Mr Temple, the whole truth and nothing but the truth, so if you don't believe me, brother, it's just too bad.

TEMPLE: (*Quickly*) I believe you, Layland! But listen! When the waiter came across to you tonight and said that I wanted – or rather, Mr Kelvin wanted – to see you in the entrance hall, did Sir Gilbert hear him?

LAYLAND: No.

TEMPLE: Are you sure of that?

LAYLAND: I – don't – think – he – did. You see, we'd more or less finished our conversation anyhow, and I was just about to leave.

TEMPLE: The conversation hadn't lasted very long, Mr Layland; I thought you were going to have dinner together?

LAYLAND: Not that I know of. He simply handed me this envelope and said: "You'll find your instructions inside, Mr Layland".

TEMPLE: Have you opened the envelope?

LAYLAND: Now, I ask you! What chance have I had to open the envelope with that cannon of yours staring me straight in the face!

TEMPLE: (*Pleasantly*) O.K. We'll dispose of the automatic …

LAYLAND: (*Opening the envelope*) There's a map in here by the look of things … I don't see any sign of the three hundred and fifty … Hello, what's this? (*Reading*) "The plane will land at approximately 8.00am at the spot marked on the enclosed map … Take the package and deliver it immediately to …"

TEMPLE: (*Continuing*) "… and deliver it immediately to St. Nicholas, Braysham. The three hundred and fifty pounds will be handed to you at St. Nicholas   …"

LAYLAND: St Nicholas … What is it – a church?

TEMPLE: I shouldn't think so. Let's have a look at the map … M'm … Braysham …

LAYLAND: Do you know the place?

TEMPLE: Fairly well. It's near Windlesea. There's a stretch of sand over on the other side of Braysham. I bet a fiver that's where the plane's going to land.

LAYLAND: Yes! Yes, it is … Look! Look! You can see it marked on the map …

TEMPLE: (*Quickly; issuing orders*) Now listen! You go straight through the village of Braysham for about a mile and a half. On the left-hand side – facing the sea – you'll see the sand dunes. The

	place – the place where the plane's due to land – is about three hundred yards up on the right. You can't mistake it, it's the only possible spot.
LAYLAND:	(*Surprised*) I say, just a minute, brother! Just a minute! Do – you – still – want – me – to – go – through – with – this – business?
TEMPLE:	Yes. I want you to collect the package from the plane and deliver it to St Nicholas.
LAYLAND:	But what is 'St Nicholas'?
TEMPLE:	I don't know; but I should imagine that the gentleman who hands over the package will probably put you wise on that point.
LAYLAND:	Yeah; but you know I'm not so sure that I want to go through with this proposition. If anything happens to me and your friends from Scotland Yard …
TEMPLE:	My friends from Scotland Yard won't interfere with you, Mr Layland – all you have to do is pick up the package from the plane, deliver it, and collect the three hundred and fifty pounds.
LAYLAND:	(*Suddenly*) O.K.! O.K., if you say so, Mr Temple!

The door opens.

TEMPLE:	What is it, Steve?
STEVE:	Paul, Sheila Baxter's just arrived, and she seems to be in rather a state about something!
TEMPLE:	(*Surprised*) Sheila Baxter?!
STEVE:	Yes – she's in the dining room.
TEMPLE:	All right! All right, Steve! Oh, and darling, ring through to Sir Graham for me – you've got the private number – tell him I want to see him at the Yard in twenty minutes.
STEVE:	In twenty minutes …
TEMPLE:	Yes …

LAYLAND:	Well, I'll beat it! Goodnight, Temple! I guess we'll meet again – pretty soon.
STEVE:	(*Puzzled*) Paul, what's happening, is Mr Layland …
TEMPLE:	I'll explain later, Steve! Now don't forget, Layland, play the whole thing perfectly straight – just the way they want it, (*Fading away; crossing with LAYLAND to the door*) It should take you about two hours to get down to Braysham, so I should leave town at about …

FADE SCENE.

Quick FADE UP: Opening of the Dining Room Door.

TEMPLE:	Hello, Miss Baxter – I'm sorry to have kept you waiting.
SHEILA:	I feel I'm making an awful nuisance of myself.
TEMPLE:	Nothing of the sort! Of course you're not making a nuisance of yourself. Hello – hasn't Steve given you a drink?
SHEILA:	(*Obviously nervous; keyed-up*) Mr Temple, please listen to me! When I left here tonight and went back to my flat, I had a strange, rather uncomfortable, sort of feeling. I felt that …
TEMPLE:	Yes?
SHEILA:	I felt that … somehow … you … didn't … believe me …
TEMPLE:	Didn't believe you, Miss Baxter?
SHEILA:	I mean, that you … didn't … believe my story about Sir Gilbert …
TEMPLE:	(*Rather puzzled*) Is that why you came back here …?

123

SHEILA:	(*Quickly*) No! No! I – I came back here because … there's … something … I ought to have told you.
TEMPLE:	About Sir Gilbert?
SHEILA:	No … No, about … myself …
TEMPLE:	Well?
SHEILA:	Mr Temple, you know what happened tonight, you know what happened downstairs, when I got out of the lift …
TEMPLE:	Yes.
SHEILA:	Well – I wasn't entirely taken by surprise.
TEMPLE:	What do you mean?
SHEILA:	I mean … that … for days now, I've thought that something like that might happen … That's why I've been so nervous and jumpy …
TEMPLE:	Why should you think that something like that might happen?
SHEILA:	Because …
TEMPLE:	Well?
SHEILA:	Because … almost everywhere I go, there's someone following me … I've known it for days now … at first, I wouldn't believe it … I thought I was imagining things, but … (*Suddenly, tensely, quickly*) this afternoon I went shopping … he followed me … the same man … I'm sure I wasn't imagining things, Mr Temple. I saw him … I saw him quite distinctly when I stopped in front of a shop window.
TEMPLE:	And you think that it was this man that attacked you … here … tonight …?
SHEILA:	Well – I – I think it must have been. He must have been waiting for me … downstairs … near the lift …

TEMPLE: What did he look like, the man that followed you this afternoon?

SHEILA: Well – I'm not very good at describing people. He was tall, stout – rather an untidy individual. He had a brown overcoat and I think he carried a pair of dirty wash-leather gloves.

TEMPLE: (*Quietly*) Did he stoop slightly, and walk rather … rather … aimlessly …?

SHEILA: (*A little surprised*) Yes … Yes, he did!

TEMPLE: (*Amused*) Well, I hardly think that he attacked you, Miss Baxter!

SHEILA: Why? Why, do you know this man?!

TEMPLE: Yes. Yes, I know him. His name's Wetherby – and he's a Superintendent at Scotland Yard.

FADE UP of MUSIC.

FADE DOWN of MUSIC.
FADE UP of SIR GRAHAM FORBES.

FORBES: I'm not sure about Steve coming along with us, Temple. It seems to me that if by any chance these people …

STEVE: There's no argument about it, Sir Graham – I'm coming! Besides, I know the Braysham district a hundred times better than you people. I was at school there for two years.

TEMPLE: (*Suddenly*) Yes. Yes, by Timothy, I forgot all about that! Well, darling, do you remember a place called 'St Nicholas'?

STEVE: 'St Nicholas'? What sort of a place?

TEMPLE: Well – I don't know.

STEVE: (*Thoughtfully*) There used to be a house called St Nicholas …

FORBES: Where?

125

STEVE: It was over on the far side of Braysham, not far from a village called Kenverton.

FORBES: This sounds like the place, Temple.

TEMPLE: Yes. What sort of a place was it, Steve?

STEVE: Oh, very large. The house stood in a kind of park – I should say the park must have been thirty or forty acres.

TEMPLE: Who did it belong to – can you remember?

STEVE: Well – in those days it used to belong to a man called Le Roy – Arthur Le Roy. But I very much doubt whether it still does.

The door is opened.

FORBES: What is it, Peters?

PETERS: (*Briskly*) I'm leaving now, sir.

FORBES: Right!

PETERS: Goodnight, Mrs Temple, I expect we shall meet later.

STEVE: Goodnight, Major.

FORBES: You know what to do, Peters, if anything goes wrong?

PETERS: Don't worry, Sir Graham, nothing's going to go wrong, not this time! (*Suddenly*) Oh … Oh, what about the Superintendent, sir?

FORBES: Wetherby's following behind. Yourself and Turner in the first car, Mr and Mrs Temple and myself in the second, and then Wetherby.

PETERS: Oh. Oh, I see. Right! Goodnight, sir!

FORBES: Goodnight, Peters.

TEMPLE: There's no doubt in your mind about the district, Major?

PETERS: There's a very big doubt, Mr Temple – in fact, I haven't the foggiest idea where the place is.

STEVE: Then how on earth do you hope to find it, if you haven't …

126

PETERS:	Sergeant Turner knows it, Mrs Temple. He knew the exact spot where the plane's likely to land the moment I mentioned Braysham.
TEMPLE:	Good!
PETERS:	Well – see you later, sir!

Door closes.

FORBES:	Well, I suppose we'd better get down, Temple. Are you driving, Temple, or would you like one of our drivers to …
TEMPLE:	Steve's driving, Sir Graham – it's her car.

Door opens.

WETHERBY:	I'm just leaving, Sir Graham.
FORBES:	Oh! Oh, we're just coming down, Wetherby.
WETHERBY:	(*Pleasantly*) Oh, good evening, Mrs Temple. Good evening, sir!
STEVE:	Good evening, Superintendent.
TEMPLE:	Hello, Wetherby. I – I was talking to quite a friend of yours this evening.
WETHERBY:	Oh? Indeed, Mr Temple?
TEMPLE:	Madame De Briac …
WETHERBY:	(*Puzzled*) Madame De Briac? (*Suddenly*) Oh – Oh, you mean Miss Baxter. That's the young lady Mr Kelvin works for.
TEMPLE:	Yes.
WETHERBY:	I've been keeping my eye on that young lady.
TEMPLE:	(*Amused*) Yes. Yes, so I hear, Superintendent. Come along, Steve.

FADE UP of MUSIC.

FADE DOWN of MUSIC.
FADE UP the sound of a car; it is travelling fairly fast; STEVE, TEMPLE and SIR GRAHAM are in the car.

TEMPLE:	What was that last place we went through?

FORBES: I think it must have been Stonedale, Temple. I noticed a signpost about …

STEVE: No, it wasn't Stonedale, Sir Graham. We don't go through Stonedale – not this way.

TEMPLE: Slow down, darling. We've plenty of time.

Pause.

FORBES: Is that clock right?

TEMPLE: No, it's about a quarter of an hour fast. It's just gone half past one.

FORBES: How far do you reckon we've got to go, Steve?

STEVE: About another fifteen miles or so, Sir Graham. If I remember rightly, there's a bridge about two or three hundred yards further on …

Pause.

FORBES: We seem to have left Wetherby behind all right …

STEVE: I noticed his headlights about ten minutes ago – just before we went through the village …

TEMPLE: Yes. Yes, so did I …

Pause.

STEVE: You can tell we're getting near the sea …

TEMPLE: Yes …

Pause.

TEMPLE: (*Quietly*) Is this Wetherby?

FORBES: Where?

TEMPLE: There's a car coming up behind, isn't there?

FORBES: I don't think so …

STEVE: Well, if there is, he hasn't got any lights.

TEMPLE: I thought I heard something …

FORBES: No. No, I don't think so.

Pause.

FORBES suddenly changes his mind.

FORBES: Yes … Yes, I think there is a car, Temple …

The sound of the second car approaching from behind is heard.

STEVE: Well, he must have switched his lights out, silly ass!

TEMPLE: Is it Wetherby?

FORBES: No. No, it's not Wetherby – although it's difficult to see …

STEVE: Well, here's the bridge, I'd better slow up or …

The sudden blare of a motor horn from the approaching car.

FORBES: Look out! He's passing you!

TEMPLE: Pull over, darling!

The car commences to overtake STEVE, then suddenly swerves.

TEMPLE: Look out! The damn fool …

FORBES: What's he trying to do!!!!

TEMPLE: (*Quickly, tensely*) Hold on, Steve! Hold tight!!! Don't let him force you over!!!!

FORBES: He's trying to force us over the bridge!

TEMPLE: Hold on, Steve! Hold on!!!! (*Suddenly, tensely*) Now – quickly! Quickly!!!! Let him have it!!!! Let him have it!!!!

There is a resounding crash as STEVE turns the wheel and smashes against the other car.

TEMPLE: Brake, Steve! Brake!!!!

FORBES: My God. He's going over the top!!!!

The car smashes over the side of the bridge and into the river.

TEMPLE: Brake!!! Brake!!! Brake, Steve!!!! For God's sake, use your brake or we'll be over the top …

FORBES: Quickly!!!!

STEVE applies the brake and with a wild, dramatic screech, the car skids to a standstill.

A tense pause.

FORBES: Phew!

TEMPLE: Are – are you all right, Steve?

STEVE: Yes … Yes … I'm all right …

FORBES: We've got to be careful how we get out of here, Temple – we're halfway over the parapet already!

TEMPLE: Yes …
FORBES: I think you'd better get out first, Temple …
TEMPLE: Yes … (*Car door opens*) … It's … all right …
             (*Feeling his way*) … the car's wedged against
             the wall … Give me your hand, Steve … Now
             be careful!

The sound of an approaching car.

FORBES: Can you manage, Steve?
STEVE: (*Climbing out of the car*) Yes …
TEMPLE: Take it steady! That's it!

The approaching car slows down and finally comes to a standstill.

FORBES: Here's Wetherby!
STEVE: (*Suddenly; shocked*) Oh, Paul – look at the
             other car … Look! … You can see the driver,
             he's …
TEMPLE: Yes, darling, don't look …

In the background, a car door slams.

FORBES: (*Concerned*) Are you feeling all right, Steve?
STEVE: Yes … Yes, don't worry, I'm O.K. …

WETHERBY arrives: excited and breathless.

WETHERBY: (*Excitedly*) Sir Graham … What happened …
             What the devil happened?
FORBES: (*With authority*) Wetherby, listen! Go down to
             the other car … You can see where the driver is
             from here … If he's not too badly hurt, get him
             up here onto the bridge … Check his identity
             and then contact our local people.
WETHERBY: Yes, very good, sir!
FORBES: I'm afraid we've got to take your car,
             Wetherby. Ready, Temple?
TEMPLE: Yes, I'm ready, Sir Graham!
FORBES: Good! Come along, Steve – we've still got to
             get to Braysham …

Quick FADE UP of MUSIC.

FADE DOWN of MUSIC.
FADE UP of a car.
FORBES: Are you sure this is the right road?
TEMPLE: Yes, it must be, Sir Graham ...
FORBES: Well, I'm not so sure, Temple! What do you think, Steve?
STEVE: Yes, it's all right, Sir Graham! Carry on, darling ... straight on ... Look, there's the sand dunes ...
FORBES: Oh ... Oh, yes ...
Pause.
FORBES: It seems hours since we left Wetherby at the bridge.
TEMPLE: I wonder if Wetherby was able to identify the ... (*Hesitates*)
FORBES: What is it?
Pause.
FORBES: What is it, Temple?
TEMPLE: (*Slowly*) I ... thought ... I ... saw ... a light on the road, as if ... (*Suddenly*) There it is!
STEVE: Somebody's flashing a torch ... He's standing in the middle of the road ...
FORBES: It's Peters! Stop, Temple!
The car slows down to a standstill.
FORBES: Hello, Peters!
The car stops.
PETERS: Hello, Sir Graham! Hello, Temple! You're rather later than I expected, sir.
FORBES: Yes – we had an accident.
TEMPLE: Have you seen Layland?
PETERS: No, sir, I haven't seen Layland, but ... (*He hesitates; something is obviously wrong*)
FORBES: But what? What's happened, Peters?

131

PETERS:	Well – the plane's here, sir – it was here when we arrived.
TEMPLE:	When you arrived?
PETERS:	Yes. There's something queer, Temple – something damn queer about the whole business.
TEMPLE:	What do you mean?
PETERS:	Well – the plane was here on the sand. It looked all right – perfectly all right – just as if he'd made a perfect landing. We found the pilot in the cockpit, sir.
FORBES:	In the cockpit? Is he there now?
PETERS:	Yes, sir. He's in a terrible condition, sir – just as if he's been beaten up or something.
TEMPLE:	Come along, let's have a look at him.
PETERS:	I don't think I'd bring Mrs Temple, sir.
TEMPLE:	No. No, you stay here, Steve, in the car.
STEVE:	Yes. Yes, all right, darling.

FADE AWAY.
FADE IN footsteps departing.

FADE UP the sound of the sea.

PETERS:	Here we are …
FORBES:	Good morning, Sergeant!
SERGEANT:	Morning, sir!
FORBES:	It's a nice-looking plane, Temple … All right, Peters – let's have a look at the pilot.
PETERS:	He's still in the cockpit, sir, because I'm afraid we haven't been able to move him …

PETERS opens the door of the plane, and the pilot can be heard moaning; he is obviously in pain.

FORBES:	(*Slowly; shocked*) Oh, good heavens … poor fellow …

A pause.

TEMPLE:	(*Quietly*) Sir Graham, I'm afraid this isn't the pilot …
FORBES:	(*Staggered*) Isn't the pilot!
PETERS:	What do you mean?
FORBES:	(*Quickly*) Then who is it?
TEMPLE:	It's Mr Layland! …

FADE UP of MUSIC.

END OF EPISODE FIVE

EPISODE SIX

IN WHICH
VALENTINE STRIKES

ANNOUNCER: Paul Temple, the celebrated novelist and private detective, is invited by Sir Graham Forbes, the Chief Commissioner of Scotland Yard, to investigate the activities of a drug smuggling organisation under the leadership of a notorious criminal known simply as – Valentine. During the course of certain investigations, Temple makes the acquaintance of a Sir Gilbert Dryden, a Miss Sheila Baxter, a Mr Charles Kelvin and an American by the name of Layland. Layland is instructed by Sir Gilbert to visit Braysham, a small village on the coast of Sussex, and to take possession of a certain package, which will be handed over to him by the pilot of the plane. Layland departs for Braysham, followed by Major Peters of the C.I.D., Sir Graham Forbes, Paul Temple and Steve.

Quick FADE UP of MUSIC.

FADE DOWN of MUSIC.
FADE Up of a car.

STEVE: Somebody's flashing a torch ... He's standing in the middle of the road ...

FORBES: It's Peters! Stop, Temple!

The car slows down to a standstill.

FORBES: Hello, Peters!

The car stops.

PETERS: Hello, Sir Graham! Hello, Temple! You're rather later than I expected, sir.

FORBES: Yes – we had an accident.

TEMPLE: Have you seen Layland?

PETERS: No, sir, I haven't seen Layland, but ... (*He hesitates; something is obviously wrong*)

137

FORBES:	But what? What's happened, Peters?
PETERS:	Well – the plane's here, sir – it was here when we arrived.
TEMPLE:	When you arrived?
PETERS:	Yes. There's something queer, Temple – something damn queer about the whole business.
TEMPLE:	What do you mean?
PETERS:	Well – the plane was here on the sand. It looked all right – perfectly all right – just as if he'd made a perfect landing. We found the pilot in the cockpit, sir.
FORBES:	In the cockpit? Is he there now?
PETERS:	Yes, sir. He's in a terrible condition, sir – just as if he's been beaten up or something.
TEMPLE:	Come along, let's have a look at him.
PETERS:	I don't think I'd bring Mrs Temple, sir.
TEMPLE:	No. No, you stay here, Steve, in the car.
STEVE:	Yes. Yes, all right, darling.

FADE AWAY.
FADE IN footsteps departing.

FADE UP the sound of the sea.

PETERS:	Here we are …
FORBES:	Good morning, Sergeant!
SERGEANT:	Morning, sir!
FORBES:	It's a nice-looking plane, Temple … All right, Peters – let's have a look at the pilot.
PETERS:	He's still in the cockpit, sir, because I'm afraid we haven't been able to move him …

PETERS opens the door of the plane, and the pilot can be heard moaning; he is obviously in pain.

| FORBES: | (*Slowly; shocked*) Oh, good heavens … poor fellow … |

138

A pause.

TEMPLE: (*Quietly*) Sir Graham, I'm afraid this isn't the pilot …

FORBES: (*Staggered*) Isn't the pilot!

PETERS: What do you mean?

FORBES: (*Quickly*) Then who is it?

TEMPLE: It's Mr Layland! …

FORBES: (*Staggered*) What!!!!

PETERS: Are you sure?

FORBES: But – but it can't be Layland!

TEMPLE: (*Quietly*) It's Layland all right … Here, give me a hand, Sir Graham … Let's have a look at him …

TEMPLE climbs into the plane.

PETERS: We've sent for an ambulance, Sir Graham, we telephoned about twenty minutes ago.

FORBES: Good.

PETERS: Of course, the hospital people believe that he's the pilot, so …

FORBES: That doesn't matter, Peters. (*Briskly*) How is he, Temple?

TEMPLE: (*On the plane*) He's in a pretty bad way, Sir Graham.

There is a sudden moan from LAYLAND as TEMPLE moves him slightly.

TEMPLE: Now, take it easy, Layland … You'll be all right, old boy …

LAYLAND: (*Terrified; tensely*) Don't touch me! Don't touch me! Leave me alone …

TEMPLE: It's all right, Layland, there's nothing to worry about …

LAYLAND: Don't hit me … Please, don't hit me …

TEMPLE: This is Temple, old boy … Paul Temple … I'm not going to hurt you …

139

LAYLAND: (*Dazed*) Temple … Temple …

FORBES: Here's a flask of brandy, Temple …

TEMPLE: Thanks … By Timothy, he's certainly taken a beating … Here we are, Layland … Try and drink this …

A moment: LAYLAND starts to drink.

TEMPLE: That's … a … good … fellow.

LAYLAND sinks back; obviously a little better for the drink.

TEMPLE: That's better …

LAYAND: (*Heavily; making an effort to talk*) Temple, listen … The plane was early … almost an hour early …the pilot was waiting for me … I … I … went down to the plane … and pretended to be O'Hara … He … He recognised me …

TEMPLE: Go on, Layland …

LAYLAND: (*With an effort*) The swine had a truncheon … a rubber truncheon … I … I … couldn't defend myself … I stood there and he … he … he hit me, Temple … He hit me!!!! He hit me!!!!

TEMPLE: (*Quietly*) Here we are … Have another drink, Leyland …

LAYLAND: (*In pain*) Oh, God, my head … It's almost bursting, I … I can't drink anymore, I …

TEMPLE: (*Softly; gently*) Come along …

LAYLAND makes an effort.

TEMPLE: That's better …

LAYLAND: (*After drinking; with almost a sigh*) Temple … Temple, if I pull through this, I've got a whole heap of things to talk to you about …

The sound of an approaching ambulance can be heard.

PETERS: Here's the ambulance, Sir Graham!

FORBES: Oh, good!

TEMPLE: Now just relax, Layland – you'll be as right as rain by tomorrow morning …

The ambulance draws near and comes to a standstill. Its engine stops.

The door of the ambulance opens.

DOCTOR: (*Briskly*) Good morning – I'm Dr West.

PETERS: Good morning, doctor.

DOCTOR: Where's the patient?

PETERS: He's in the cockpit.

DOCTOR: (*Obviously puzzled*) Oh. Oh, I see. Are you the gentleman that telephoned?

PETERS: No. Sergeant Turner – here – telephoned you. My name is Peters – and this is Sir Graham Forbes, C.I.D.

FORBES: Good morning, doctor!

DOCTOR: (*Impressed*) Oh. Oh, good morning, Sir Graham! Well, what's happened exactly?

FORBES: There's been an accident. We want you to get this man to hospital as quickly as possible.

DOCTOR: Oh. Oh, I see. (*Makes his mind up*) All right – we'll have a look at him.

DR WEST climbs into the plane.

TEMPLE: Can you see all right?

DOCTOR: Yes. I say, he is in a pretty bad way, isn't he? (*He touches LAYLAND's head*) Does that hurt you, old man?

LAYLAND: (*Tensely; almost frightened again*) Don't touch me … Don't touch me …

DOCTOR: (*Softly*) O.K. (*Calling down*) I shall want my case, Nurse – I'm going to give an injection.

NURSE: Yes, very good, doctor.

DOCTOR: You'll find it on the front seat.

NURSE: Yes, doctor …

LAYLAND: (*Tensely; frightened*) Don't touch me! Please don't touch me!

DOCTOR: (*Quietly, aside to TEMPLE*) He'll be all right when we get him to the hospital.

FORBES: You'd better go back to the hospital with the doctor, Peters – then if Layland recovers and starts talking, we shall have somebody on hand.

PETERS: Yes, all right, Sir Graham.

NURSE: (*Handing over the case*) Here we are, doctor.

DOCTOR: Thank you, Nurse … (*Opening the case*) Now … this … isn't … going … to … hurt … you … so … don't … (*He is fixing a syringe*) … get … nervous …

LAYLAND: What – what are you going to do? Don't touch me! Don't …

The DOCTOR gives the injection.

LAYLAND: Oh … (*Weakly*) Oh …

DOCTOR: (*Quietly*) Now, if you'll give me a hand, sir, we'll get him down to the ambulance …

TEMPLE: Yes, certainly …

TEMPLE and the DOCTOR move LAYLAND from the plane.

DOCTOR: Careful … Careful …

TEMPLE: Watch his head, will you?

FORBES: Do you want any help, Temple, or …

TEMPLE: No … it's … all right … I think we can manage …

DOCTOR: That's right, Nurse, get the stretcher on the ground so that we can … (*Lowering LAYLAND*) That's it … That's fine … Steady, sir … Steady … There we are … Good!

FORBES: Sergeant, take Major Peters' car and report back to Braysham – you'll probably find Superintendent Wetherby there.

SERGEANT: Very good, sir.

FORBES: And keep the radio going, Sergeant – just in case we need you.

SERGEANT:	Yes, sir.
PETERS:	(*Confidentially*) But what about the pilot, sir – he must still be somewhere in the district!
FORBES:	We'll look for the pilot, Peters – you keep your eye on Layland. It's my guess that when he comes to his senses, he'll spill the beans – so far as tonight's concerned, at any rate.
TEMPLE:	I shouldn't be surprised, Sir Graham. Watch him, Peters – stay with him all the time – don't let the hospital people frighten you away.

The ambulance starts up.

PETERS:	Leave that to me, sir.
NURSE:	We're ready now, sir!
PETERS:	Yes, very good, Nurse.
FORBES:	Oh, doctor – do you know of a house round here called St Nicholas?
NURSE:	St Nicholas? Yes, it's near Kenverton.
FORBES:	Thank you. (*Aside, to TEMPLE*) Steve was obviously right.
TEMPLE:	Yes. Come along, Sir Graham, let's go back to the car.

FADE SCENE.

FADE UP of TEMPLE and FORBES arriving at the car. TEMPLE opens the car door.

TEMPLE:	… Did you think we were never coming, Steve?
STEVE:	(*Quickly*) What's happened? I saw the ambulance drive past …
TEMPLE:	They've taken Layland to the hospital.
STEVE:	(*Astonished*) Layland! But I thought Major Peters said that it was the pilot of the plane …
TEMPLE:	Major Peters made a mistake – quite a natural one, I'm afraid.
STEVE:	What do you mean?

TEMPLE: Layland was beaten up by the pilot and placed in the cockpit.

STEVE: Then what's happened to the pilot?

TEMPLE: Your guess is as good as ours!

FORBES: Well, my guess is that when he realised that Layland wasn't O'Hara and consequently – from his point of view – couldn't be trusted, he …

TEMPLE: He what, Sir Graham?

FORBES: He made up his mind that the best thing he could do was to deliver the package himself.

STEVE: To the house known as St Nicholas?

FORBES: Yes.

TEMPLE: (*Quietly*) I wonder …

FORBES: But dash it all, Temple – he must have done!

STEVE: Why, of course, darling!

TEMPLE: Sir Graham, listen! Layland's tough – he's as tough as nails. I'd back Layland against anybody in a straight fight. But tonight – or rather this morning – if you want my opinion – it wasn't a   straight fight.

FORBES: (*Faintly irritated*) Yes. Yes, we know that. He obviously started to do his O'Hara impersonation – the pilot saw through it – and realised he wasn't O'Hara and …

STEVE: Let him have it!

FORBES: Exactly!

TEMPLE: And you really think that's what happened?

FORBES: Of course that's what happened! Layland as good as said so!

TEMPLE: (*Emphatically*) Yes – well – I'm glad you think so! Because I don't!

FORBES: What do you mean?

STEVE: What do you think happened, darling?

TEMPLE: I think the pilot arrived, delivered the package, and then came back here and waited for Layland.

144

In other words, he never even expected O'Hara – he was forewarned.

FORBES: You mean, that they knew all the time that Layland was playing in with us?

TEMPLE: Yes.

FORBES: (*Impressed*) I hadn't thought of that …

TEMPLE: Don't you see, that's why the pilot was able to take Layland completely by surprise! He never ever expected O'Hara …

STEVE: (*A sudden thought, yet quietly*) But Paul …

TEMPLE: (*Quietly*) Yes, Steve?

STEVE: If they know that we know the truth about Layland, then they also know that …

TEMPLE: That we know about the house – St Nicholas. Yes …

FORBES: (*A sudden realisation*) Now I see what you're getting at! In other words, they expect us to go to the house – in other words … they're … waiting … for … us!

TEMPLE: (*Quietly*) Yes.

FORBES: (*Thoughtfully*) And I'd have fallen for it!

TEMPLE: I'm afraid you would have done, Sir Graham.

STEVE: (*Quietly*) Then this means that we don't go to the house after all, darling …

TEMPLE: If we want to see this thing through, we've got to go to the house, Steve. But …

FORBES: But what …?

TEMPLE: (*Quietly*) … We go with our eyes open …

FADE UP of MUSIC.

FADE DOWN of MUSIC.
FADE UP two cars. They stop.
WETHERBY: Hello, Sergeant! Where are you off to?

145

SERGEANT: Sir Graham told me to report back to Braysham, sir. He said I should probably bump into you.

WETHERBY: How is Sir Graham, Sergeant?

SERGEANT: He seems all right, sir. Why?

WETHERBY: There was a terrific accident a few miles back – a man called Lefty Stoner tried to force them over a bridge.

SERGEANT: Well, they didn't seem any the worse for it, sir.

WETHERBY: That's more than I can say for Stoner, I'm afraid.

SERGEANT: Where did you get the car from, Superintendent?

WETHERBY: It belongs to the local people. If you follow me back to the village, I'll change over.

SERGEANT: Yes, I think you'd better, sir. Sir Graham told me to keep the radio going.

A car approaches.

WETHERBY: Hello, who's this coming along?

SERGEANT: It's probably the ambulance, sir.

WETHERBY: The ambulance? Who's in it?

SERGEANT: Layland. They're taking him to hospital.

WETHERBY: Was he hurt or something?

SERGEANT: He was beaten up, sir.

WETHERBY: Oh. Is there anyone else in the ambulance beside Layland?

SERGEANT: Major Peters, sir.

WETHERBY: Major Peters? Oh! I'd like a word with him.

SERGEANT: Well – here you are, sir, you'd better stop them.

WETHERBY: Give me a torch, will you?

The car pulls up.

SERGEANT: It's not the ambulance.

WETHERBY: Good heavens no.

KELVIN: What's the matter here – is the road up or something?

WETHERBY: No – I'm sorry, I was under the impression that – Just a minute – aren't you Mr Kelvin?

KELVIN: Yes.

WETHERBY: Good evening, Mr Kelvin. What are you doing here – visiting relations?

FADE UP of MUSIC.

FADE DOWN of MUSIC.
FADE UP of a gale; wild and violent; through the gale FADE UP slowly the noise of a car.

FORBES: What a filthy night! I don't know how you're managing to keep the car on the road, Temple!

TEMPLE: More by luck than judgement, I'm afraid.

STEVE: There's a corner here, darling – take it steady.

The car slows down and turns the corner.

FORBES: How much further, Steve?

STEVE: Well – it can't be very much further. We've passed Kenverton …

A pause.
The gale dies down slightly.

TEMPLE: (*Quietly*) Hello – what's this place on the top of the hill …

STEVE: (*Quickly*) That's it! That's it – St Nicholas!

The car slows down.

FORBES: M'm – pretty impressive sort of place …

TEMPLE: By Timothy, it certainly is!

STEVE: Looks more like a medieval castle than anything else …

TEMPLE: Yes … reminds me of that place at Inverdale … Skerry Lodge …

STEVE: That's just what I was thinking!

FORBES: Doesn't appear to be a light showing …

TEMPLE: No.

The car slows down to a standstill.

STEVE: (*A little surprised*) What are you stopping the car for?

TEMPLE: What did you expect me to do, darling – drive straight up to the front door?

STEVE: No, but you can get much nearer than this, Paul – the drive's about a hundred yards long.

TEMPLE: This is quite near enough, my sweet – for the time being.

A car door opens.

TEMPLE: No, don't get out, Sir Graham, I'm going to park the car on the side of the road.

The car door closes.

FORBES: There's a good spot over there, Temple, near that gate.

TEMPLE: Yes.

TEMPLE draws the car into the side and switches off the engine.

STEVE: Now what do we do? Simply stroll up the drive?

TEMPLE: We? You stay here, darling – in the car.

STEVE: What?

TEMPLE: You'll be far more use to us here, Steve, than you will be up at the house.

FORBES: I quite agree.

TEMPLE: Give us about half an hour, Steve. Then, if you don't see a light from one of the windows – you know the signal, darling, we've used it before – contact Sergeant Turner.

STEVE: Yes, all right.

FORBES: You know how to work this radio, Steve?

STEVE: Yes, I think so.

FORBES switches on the transmitting set; there is a certain amount of whistling and oscillation before he connects with the voice of SERGEANT TURNER.

SERGEANT: Calling car DH0 838 ... Calling car DH0 838 ... Calling car DH0 838 ...

FORBES: (*A click of switch-over*) Hello, Sergeant! Contact! Over to you ... (*Click*)

SERGEANT: Superintendent Wetherby's here, Sir Graham.

FORBES: (*Click*) Oh, is he? Good!

TEMPLE: I'd like a word with Wetherby.

FORBES: Put the Superintendent on, Sergeant. (*Click*)

WETHERBY: (*In an official manner*) Superintendent Wetherby reporting, sir.

TEMPLE: (*Click*) This is Temple, Superintendent. Were you able to identify the man with the car – the man who tried to force us over the bridge? (*Click*)

WETHERBY: Yes. I had confirmation through from the Yard about five minutes ago. His name was Stoner – Lefty Stoner. (*Click*)

TEMPLE: Did he talk? (*Click*)

WETHERBY: He was dead when I reached him. (*Click*)

TEMPLE: Oh. Oh, I see. Right! (*Click*)

WETHERBY: I've got another little surprise for you, Temple. We've picked up Charles Kelvin. (*Click*)

TEMPLE: Have you, Wetherby? That's interesting! Here's the Commissioner ...

FORBES: Wetherby, I want you to telephone through to Major Peters at the hospital. If Layland's been able to give Peters a description of the pilot, contact the car straight away. (*Click*)

WETHERBY: Yes, sir. (*A moment*) Will you be there, sir? (*Click*)

FORBES:	No – we're just outside Kenverton, near the house called St Nicholas … (*Click*)
WETHERBY:	Oh. (*He understands*) Oh, I see, sir. (*Click*)
FORBES:	But Mrs Temple's staying in the car – keep in contact. (*Click*)
WETHERBY:	Very good, sir. (*Click*)
FORBES:	Goodbye, Wetherby! (*Final switch off*)
TEMPLE:	Ready, Sir Graham?

TEMPLE opens his car door.

FORBES:	Yes, I'm ready …
STEVE:	(*Anxiously*) Take care, darling …

Quick FADE UP of MUSIC.

FADE DOWN of MUSIC.
FADE UP the noise of the wind in the trees; the occasional hooting of an owl; the sound of a dog barking. TEMPLE and FORBES are approaching the house. They are moving softly, stealthily.

FORBES:	(*A quick whisper*) Where's the dog?
TEMPLE:	It's all right – I think it's over on the other side.
FORBES:	(*Breathlessly*) Let's wait here a minute … We're in the shadow … Stand near the tree.
TEMPLE:	Ten to one they've spotted us by now …
FORBES:	I don't know … There isn't any light showing … (*He is getting his breath back*)
TEMPLE:	Are you O.K.?
FORBES:	Yes … Yes, I'm all right now …
TEMPLE:	Now don't forget what I've told you, Sir Graham … Have you got the revolver?
FORBES:	Yes …
TEMPLE:	Keep me covered – and don't move until you see the torch.

FORBES: All right, but I still think you're taking a risk, Temple, simply walking across the lawn towards the house like that.

TEMPLE: If they're watching us – they won't know what I'm up to ... They'll be curious ... I'm pretty sure they won't do anything, not at first ... (*A moment*) O.K.! O.K. I'm off ...

FORBES: Watch yourself! (*Softly*) I've got you covered ...

TEMPLE commences to whistle, quite openly and cheerfully, and saunters across the lawn towards the house.

FADE SCENE on TEMPLE whistling.

FADE UP of TEMPLE whistling. He arrives at the house and pulls the old-fashioned bell pull. We hear the bell clanging away at the back of the house. The dog howls. TEMPLE pulls the bell pull again. Pause. The sound of the bell again. A moment. TEMPLE uses the door knocker.

TEMPLE: Hello there!!!! Hello!!!! (*He vigorously uses both the knocker and the bell pull*) Hello, there!!!!

TEMPLE repeats the bell and knocker. The dog howls. The sound of the bell, and the noise created by the knocking dies down. The dog stops howling.

TEMPLE: M'm ... (*Softly*) M'm ...

A pause.

SIR GRAHAM arrives.

FORBES: Well, if they can't hear that, they can't hear anything! I thought you were trying to wake the dead!

TEMPLE: I'm not so sure that we're not barking up the wrong tree, Sir Graham ...

FORBES: You mean – the house is empty?

TEMPLE: It's beginning to look like it.

FORBES: Have you tried the door?

TEMPLE: Yes – it's locked.

151

FORBES: Looks pretty solid to me. We'd never break that down, even if we wanted to.

TEMPLE: What about the window over there?

FORBES: (*Suddenly*) Oh, yes! (*A pause; he tries the window*)

TEMPLE: Is it unlatched?

Pause.

FORBES: (*Forcing the window*) … It is now …

TEMPLE: (*Laughing; softly*) Good!

FORBES: (*Pushing open the window*) Give me a leg up, Temple!

TEMPLE: Can you make it, Sir Graham?

FORBES: Yes … Yes, I can make it all right! (*He climbs onto the windowsill; helped by TEMPLE*) O.K. …

TEMPLE: Watch you don't fall backwards.

FORBES: I'm all right … (*He pushes open the window and enters the room*)

TEMPLE: Give me your hand! (*TEMPLE takes SIR GRAHAM's hand and climbs onto the windowsill*)

FORBES: Steady! That's it!

With a little jump, TEMPLE springs into the room.

FORBES: Nice work!

TEMPLE: (*After a pause; taking stock*) Well, this part of the house looks completely deserted – it isn't even furnished.

FORBES: No. (*A moment; puzzled*) Do you smell anything Temple?

TEMPLE: No … No, I don't think so … Why?

FORBES: (*Vaguely; uncertain*) Oh, I thought I could … I noticed it outside …

TEMPLE: I can't smell anything … (*A moment*) It's a pretty big room this, isn't it?

FORBES: Yes … Looks to me as if it might have been the library …

TEMPLE: (*Quietly*) Let's have a look at the rest of the house
    …

TEMPLE and FORBES pass out into the hall.

FORBES: This place isn't quite so impressive inside as out …

TEMPLE: No … No, it certainly isn't …

FORBES: That staircase is pretty dilapidated – it looks to
    me as if it's falling to pieces …

TEMPLE: (*Slowly, watchfully*) You know, I've got a hunch
    we're in for rather a surprise, Sir Graham. I don't
    know what it is, but …

FORBES: (*Quickly*) Listen!

Pause.

TEMPLE: What is it?

FORBES: Don't you hear anything?

TEMPLE: No …

FORBES: (*Softly; tensely*) Listen …

From above can be heard a soft, low moan …

FORBES: Now do you hear it?

TEMPLE: Yes … It's upstairs …

The noise is repeated.

FORBES: What is it?

TEMPLE: I don't know … but whatever it is, it's in the house
    …

A pause.

FORBES: I don't hear it now …

TEMPLE: No … it's stopped … (*Quietly*) Let's go upstairs …

TEMPLE and FORBES start to climb the staircase.

FORBES: I wonder how many floors there are …?

TEMPLE: I don't know … I should say there are certainly
    three …

The staircase creaks.

TEMPLE: By Timothy, you were right about this staircase …

FORBES: The wood's absolutely rotten … (*He stops*)

We hear the noise again; a low, soft moan.

TEMPLE: It sounds to me as if someone's gagged, and …

FORBES: (*Quickly*) … And they're trying to make themselves heard? That's exactly what it sounds like!

TEMPLE: (*Grimly*) Come on!

TEMPLE and FORBES climb the staircase.

FADE IN of MUSIC.

FADE DOWN of MUSIC.

The noise is nearer.

FORBES: (*Slightly breathless*) I think it's on the top floor …

TEMPLE: No … No, I don't think so … (*He moves away from FORBES*) It seems to me … to … be over here …

The noise is louder.

FORBES: Yes, I think you're right … (*He joins TEMPLE*) Is there a room here …?

TEMPLE: I don't know … Where's that torch? …

FORBES: Here we are … It's all right, I'll hold it!

TEMPLE: (*Quickly*) Yes … Yes, there's a door! …

TEMPLE tries the door; it is locked. As he tries the door, the noise from inside the room is much louder.

TEMPLE: This is it, all right … There's someone in there …

FORBES: Is it locked?

TEMPLE: (*Quickly; keyed up*) Yes … (*He knocks on the door*) Can you hear me? Can you hear me in there?

The person inside the room struggles to answer; they are obviously gagged.

FORBES: You were right, Temple – they're obviously gagged and …

TEMPLE: (*Suddenly*) Look out, there! I'm breaking the door down!!! (*He throws his full weight against the door, smashing the panel to pieces*) Show a light, Sir Graham!!!! Quickly!!!

The door bursts open.

FORBES: (*Staggered*) Why, Temple ….!!!!

TEMPLE: (*Equally astonished*) By Timothy! It's Major Peters!!!!

Quick, dramatic flourish of music.

Quick FADE DOWN of MUSIC.

FORBES: (*Stunned*) Peters, what the devil are you doing here?

TEMPLE: (*Quickly*) You untie his legs, Sir Graham – I'll ungag him!

TEMPLE and FORBES release PETERS.

PETERS: (*Weakly*) Thank heavens you heard me! Oh … Oh, my head! …

FORBES: (*Bewildered*) But, Peters, how did you get here? We thought you were at the hospital with Layland!

TEMPLE: (*Ominously*) You don't have to ask that question, Sir Graham …

PETERS: That swine wasn't a doctor at all – as soon as we got out onto the open road, they let me have it! God knows what they hit me with! (*Wincing*) Oh, my head! You haven't got any of that brandy left, have you, Sir Graham?

FORBES: Yes … Yes – here we are …

PETERS: Thanks … (*He drinks*)

TEMPLE: (*Thoughtfully; yet to FORBES*) You can see what happened. They wanted to get Layland away before he gave us a description of the pilot. They must have been on the verge of getting him away   when Peters first arrived. They pushed him into the cockpit, and waited – then when the ambulance turned up, they waylaid the ambulance and drove down to the … (*He hesitates*)

FORBES: (*Anxiously*) What is it? (*Quickly*) Temple, what is it?

TEMPLE: Sir Graham! What did you think you could smell – when you were downstairs?

155

FORBES: (*Puzzled*) I don't know …

TEMPLE: Was it methylated spirits?

FORBES: It might have been …

PETERS: (*Suddenly*) Temple, listen!

FORBES: (*Quickly*) I can smell burning!!! You don't mean that they've set the place on fire!

TEMPLE: Wait here!!! Wait here, Sir Graham!

TEMPLE dashes out onto the landing. The lower part of the house is already on fire; the fire is spreading.

FORBES: (*Joining TEMPLE*) They must have watched us … They must have watched us and waited until we got upstairs …

TEMPLE: Yes …

FORBES: Temple – we'll never get down that staircase!

TEMPLE: It'll burn like matchwood!!!

FADE UP of the fire spreading from the floor below.

PETERS: What are we going to do?

TEMPLE: I'm afraid there's only one thing we can do, we've got to go down the staircase …

FORBES: We'll never make it, Temple!!!!

FADE UP of the fire.

PETERS: I agree with Sir Graham – it's quite impossible …

TEMPLE: (*Taking stock of the situation*) Well, if we don't go down the staircase, I'm afraid we're sunk!

The fire suddenly swells up and part of the staircase collapses.

TEMPLE: By Timothy!

FORBES: That's torn it!

PETERS: We'll have to try and get out onto the roof, there's a window over here and …

TEMPLE: (*Quickly*) Where? Where?!

PETERS: Here we are … It's over here! (*Suddenly*) Hello!

FORBES: What is it?

PETERS: There's a car coming up the drive!

The sound of a car.

156

TEMPLE: It must be Steve!

FORBES: Yes!

TEMPLE: Look out, Peters!!! (*He smashes the window*)

FADE UP of the fire and falling masonry.

FORBES: (*Shouting down*) Steve!!!! Steve!!!!

The sound of a second car.

PETERS: (*Excitedly*) If only we had a rope …

TEMPLE: There's another car! It's Wetherby and Sergeant Turner!

FORBES: Wetherby must have telephoned the hospital, realised that Peters wasn't there and then contacted … (*Suddenly, alarmed*) Look out, Peters!!!!

FADE UP of fire; another part of the staircase collapses.

TEMPLE: Stand over here, Peters … For the love of Mike, don't stand too near the staircase …

WETHERBY: (*Shouting from below*) Where are you? Where are you, Temple?

FORBES: (*Excitedly; tensely*) Can't he see us?

TEMPLE: (*Shouting*) We're over here, Wetherby!!!!

FORBES: Over here!!!!

PETERS: (*Excitedly; alarmed*) You can do what you like, Temple; I'm going upstairs onto the next floor before this confounded place collapses!

TEMPLE: (*Suddenly*) Wait a minute!!!!

WETHERBY: (*Calling from below*) Temple!!!

TEMPLE: What is it?!!!

WETHERBY: I've got a rope! Get ready to catch it!!!!

FORBES: Good man!!!!

TEMPLE: Look out! Here it comes!!!

WETHERBY throws the rope. It smashes against the broken window.

FORBES: Damn! He's missed it!

TEMPLE: (*Shouting down*) Try again!!!!

WETHERBY throws the rope up again.

FORBES: Here it comes! Here it ... (*He holds his breath*)

A gasp from TEMPLE, FORBES and PETERS.

FORBES: Good man!!!!

PETERS: Well done, Temple! You've got it!!!!

TEMPLE: (*Briskly*) Come on, Peters! Quickly! Out you
             go ...

PETERS: No, you go first, Temple! There's no reason
             why I should be the ...

TEMPLE: Come on, Peters!!! Don't argue! This isn't
             chapter two of the Boys Own Paper! We're in a
             spot – one hell of a spot – and we want to get
             out of it!

FORBES: You said it, Temple! Come on, Peters!!!!

PETERS: O.K.!

*FADE UP of the fire; it is spreading rapidly; the noise of
falling masonry, etc.*

FADE IN MUSIC.

FADE noise of the fire, falling masonry, etc, to the background.

STEVE: (*Anxiously; worried*) I hope he'll be all right ...
             (*Raising her voice*) Darling, do be careful!

FORBES: He'll be all right, Steve! (*Raising his voice*)
             Watch the rope at the top, Temple!

A pause.

PETERS: (*Shouting*) Watch it, Temple! Don't rush it!

WETHERBY: I wonder what he's tied the rope to?

PETERS: I don't know, there didn't appear to be ... (*He
             stops*)

STEVE: (*Nervously*) Oh ... Oh ... (*Alarmed*) Ooh ...

*There is a sudden, quick, frightened gasp from FORBES,
STEVE, PETERS and WETHERBY – and then a quick gasp of
relief ...*

WETHERBY: Phew! I thought he'd had it!

PETERS:	So did I!
FORBES:	(*Softly*) Don't worry, Steve – he'll make it all right – He's over the worst part now!

A pause.

PETERS:	(*To himself; watching*) Here he comes …
FORBES:	(*Watching; a moment*) Good man …

TEMPLE jumps to the ground.

STEVE:	(*Rushing towards TEMPLE*) Oh, darling … darling …
TEMPLE:	(*Laughing, out of breath*) It's all right, Steve … It's all right … (*Laughing*) … I feel exactly like Gary Cooper … (*They all laugh*) Are you any better, Peters?
PETERS:	Yes, I feel much better now …
TEMPLE:	Good …
FORBES:	I suppose you telephoned the hospital, Wetherby, and discovered that Peters hadn't arrived?
WETHERBY:	Yes. That's exactly what happened, sir!
TEMPLE:	You said you picked up Kelvin? Where is he?
WETHERBY:	He's in the car, sir – with the Sergeant.
FORBES:	(*Quietly*) Let's have a word with him, Temple.

FADE SCENE.

FADE UP of a car door opening.

SERGEANT:	(*Briskly*) Good morning, sir!
FORBES:	Good morning, Sergeant!
KELVIN:	(*Quickly; impulsively*) Mr Temple … Mr Temple, please don't let them take me back to Town … I can explain everything! Honestly, I can … I … I …
TEMPLE:	(*Quietly*) Can you, Kelvin?
FORBES:	(*Sharply*) What are you doing here?

159

KELVIN: (*Hesitant; uncertain of himself*) I … I came down here because … because Sir Gilbert Dryden told me that … (*He hesitates*)

TEMPLE: That what?

KELVIN: Sir Gilbert told me that if I came down to Braysham … if I came down to Braysham and met a friend of his called … Mr Layland … he … he would pay me … a hundred pounds.

TEMPLE: (*Quietly*) Did you meet Mr Layland?

KELVIN: No … No, I've never seen the gentleman …

TEMPLE: Never seen the gentleman? Now that's interesting, Mr Kelvin …

KELVIN: What do you mean?

TEMPLE: Didn't you persuade Mr Layland to impersonate a certain Captain O'Hara? Didn't you?!

KELVIN: Most certainly not!

TEMPLE: Didn't you persuade Mr Layland to meet me at a public house … a public house known as The Marquis of Bude?

KELVIN: (*Nervously*) Of course not. I … (*He is feeling in his pocket*) … I've already told you I've never even seen … (*He makes a sudden, unexpected move and produces a revolver*)

TEMPLE: (*Suddenly; tensely*) Look out! Look out, Sir Graham! He's got a gun!

SERGEANT: (*Quickly; annoyed*) Why you cunning little …

The revolver goes off in the struggle and smashes the windscreen of the car; there is a smack and a groan from KELVIN as he falls forward in the car.

TEMPLE: Nice work, Sergeant!

SERGEANT: I'm sorry about the revolver, sir – but I did search him …

FORBES: (*Quietly*) That's all right, Sergeant – take him back
　　　　to town …
FADE UP of MUSIC.

Slow FADE DOWN of MUSIC.
A tiny bedside clock chimes the half hour. TEMPLE yawns and
stretches himself.
STEVE:　　(*Sleepy; only just awake*) What time is it?
TEMPLE: (*Yawning*) It's … just … gone ... half past eleven …
STEVE:　　Good gracious!
TEMPLE: It's all right – we didn't get to bed till half past six.
There is a knock, and the door opens.
MARY:　　Are ye awake?
STEVE:　　Yes – come in, Mary!
MARY:　　I've brought ye both a nice cup o' tea – not that
　　　　ye deserve it now, coming in at that time o' the
　　　　morning!
TEMPLE: What sort of a day is it?
MARY:　　It's a very nice day … (*Suddenly, remembering*)
　　　　Oh! Oh, before I forget! … There's a young lady to
　　　　see you, she's in the lounge … A Miss Baxter …
TEMPLE: Miss Baxter? Yes, all right, Mary … (*Aside*) Pass
　　　　me that dressing gown, darling …
FADE.

FADE UP.
A door opens.
TEMPLE: (*Pleasantly*) I'm sorry to have kept you waiting,
　　　　Miss Baxter. Oh, dear! Didn't Mary offer you some
　　　　coffee?
SHEILA: (*Nervously; tensely*) Mr Temple … Mr Temple,
　　　　forgive me calling at this … at this time of the
　　　　morning, but …
TEMPLE: That's all right, Miss Baxter.

161

SHEILA: … but I think I've got some rather important news
          for you …
TEMPLE: Oh? (*A moment*) Oh, indeed?
There is a slight pause.
SHEILA: (*Almost with emotion*) I know the … identity … of
          … Valentine …

END OF EPISODE SIX

EPISODE SEVEN

IN WHICH
THE NET TIGHTENS

ANNOUNCER: Paul Temple, the celebrated novelist and private detective, is invited by Sir Graham Forbes, the Chief Commissioner of Scotland Yard, to investigate the activities of a drug smuggling organisation under the leadership of a notorious criminal known simply as – Valentine. Whilst working on the case – with Superintendent Wetherby and Major Peters – Temple makes the acquaintance of a Sir Gilbert Dryden and a Mr Charles Kelvin. Dryden tells Temple that he suspects the leader of the organisation – Valentine – is a protegé of his, a girl called Sheila Baxter. Sheila Baxter is the proprietor of a Beauty Salon in the West End of London and is known professionally as Madame De Briac. (*Start to FADE*) One morning, Sheila Baxter visits Paul Temple …

FADE UP.
A door opens.
TEMPLE: (*Pleasantly*) I'm sorry to have kept you waiting, Miss Baxter. Oh, dear! Didn't Mary offer you some coffee?
SHEILA: (*Nervously; tensely*) Mr Temple … Mr Temple, forgive me calling at this … at this time of the morning, but …
TEMPLE: That's all right, Miss Baxter.
SHEILA: … but I think I've got some rather important news for you …
TEMPLE: Oh? (*A moment*) Oh, indeed?
There is a slight pause.
SHEILA: (*Almost with emotion*) I know the … identity … of … Valentine …

165

TEMPLE: Valentine? Are you sure?

SHEILA: Yes … Yes, I'm absolutely sure! (*Almost a shade distressed*) My suspicions were justified, Mr Temple!

TEMPLE: You mean that …

SHEILA: (*Distressed; with an effort*) I mean that Sir Gilbert Dryden is Valentine …

TEMPLE: (*A moment; then suddenly*) Dryden? Sit down! Sit down, Miss Baxter! (*A slight pause*) Now what makes you so certain that Sir Gilbert is Valentine? When you saw my wife the other day you said, if I remember correctly, …

SHEILA: Something's happened, Mr Temple! Something happened this morning which utterly and completely convinces me that Sir Gilbert is Valentine …

TEMPLE: Go on …

SHEILA: About an hour ago, I received a telephone message. I was asked to go round and see Sir Gilbert at his house in Berkeley Square …

TEMPLE: Yes …

SHEILA: When I arrived at the house, Sir Gilbert was in the study – he wanted to see me about a private matter, as a matter of fact, about some shares which I inherited from my father. We were talking about the shares when suddenly …

TEMPLE: Yes?

SHEILA: … when suddenly the telephone rang. As soon as Sir Gilbert answered the phone, I knew that something was the matter. He was on edge, nervous, jumpy, rather – rather annoyed about something. Suddenly, without speaking a word, he put the telephone receiver down on the desk and walked through to the drawing room.

There's an extension in the drawing room, so I knew that …

TEMPLE: That he wanted to talk privately?

SHEILA: Yes.

TEMPLE: Go on, Miss Baxter …

SHEILA: Well – to cut a long story short – I picked up the receiver and … and … overheard the conversation …

TEMPLE: (*A moment; quietly*) Go on …

SHEILA: Mr Temple – Mr Temple, do you know who it was on the telephone?

TEMPLE: No ….

SHEILA: It was a man called Condré – Jules Condré. I'd never heard of him before, but I could tell immediately what they were talking about. Apparently, this man Condré had just arrived from the Continent with a certain package. He told Sir Gilbert that he hadn't the slightest intention of handing over the package until he received the sum of six hundred pounds.

TEMPLE: Did this man Condré seem annoyed – irritated?

SHEILA: Extremely annoyed! He told Sir Graham that he knew exactly what had happened to a friend of his, a certain Captain … Captain …?

TEMPLE: O'Hara?

SHEILA: Yes!

TEMPLE: (*Most intrigued*) Go on …

SHEILA: From what I could gather, this man Condré had only just arrived in the country. He spoke as if he'd flown over from France in the early hours of this morning … He mentioned a place called … now what was it? … (*Suddenly*) Braysham!

TEMPLE: Go on … Go on, Miss Baxter …

SHEILA: Well – although he never actually referred to
              Sir Graham as Valentine, it was quite obvious
              from the conversation, that he looked upon him
              as the leader of some sort of an organisation.
              He told Sir Gilbert that he would deliver the
              package tonight if Sir Gilbert would agree to
              hand over the six hundred pounds.

TEMPLE: (*Quickly*) What did Dryden say?

SHEILA: He told Condré to meet him at seven o'clock.

TEMPLE: Where? At Berkeley Square?

SHEILA: No … Condré wanted to come to the house, but
              Sir Gilbert wouldn't hear of it. He told him to
              meet him on platform No 3 …

TEMPLE: Platform No 3? (*Quickly*) Which platform No
              3?

SHEILA: (*Nervously; she is almost frightened by the
              interest TEMPLE is taking in her story*)   Now
              … Now just a minute! … Let me get this
              straight … Condré said … (*Recalling the
              conversation*) … "If you don't want to see me
              at the house, where do you want to see me? …"
              And Sir Gilbert said … "Meet me on the
              Underground … Platform 3 … Piccadilly Tube
              Station … Tonight at …" …

TEMPLE: At seven o'clock?

SHEILA: Yes …

TEMPLE: (*The final word, manner*) Thank you, Miss
              Baxter!

SHEILA: Oh, Mr Temple – I do hope I'm wrong about
              Sir Gilbert. I know he's changed – changed a
              great deal in the last two or three years, but …

TEMPLE: (*Not listening to SHEILA*) Miss Baxter, tell me:
              was this a trunk call – the one Sir Gilbert
              received from Condré?

SHEILA: Yes. Yes, I think it was. At any rate I heard the pips. (*Suddenly*) Mr Temple, do you think I ought to have gone to Scotland Yard about this matter, I mean …

TEMPLE: No … No, you did the right thing, Miss Baxter, in coming to see me – now don't you worry about anything.

The door opens.

STEVE: (*Brightly; pushing a tea trolley*) Hello, Miss Baxter!

SHEILA: Hello, Mrs Temple …

STEVE: We're just having some tea – wouldn't you like a cup?

SHEILA: Well …

TEMPLE: Of course she would!

The telephone rings.

TEMPLE: It's all right, darling – I'll take that in the study.

FADE DOWN of the telephone bell.

The door opens and closes as TEMPLE enters the study.

FADE UP the bell in the study as TEMPLE crosses to the desk.

He lifts the receiver.

TEMPLE: (*On the phone*) Hello?

SERGEANT: (*On the other end; slightly cockney*) Mr Temple?

TEMPLE: Yes …

SERGEANT: Hold the line, sir. Sir Graham wants you. (*Aside*) You're through, sir!

FORBES: Hello, Temple?

TEMPLE: Hello, Sir Graham!

FORBES: Temple, listen! We're having a conference this afternoon – three o'clock – I'd rather like you to be there if you can manage it.

TEMPLE: Yes … Yes, that's all right, Sir Graham.

FORBES: Good!

TEMPLE: Any new developments?

FORBES: (*Cautiously*) Well – I've been in touch with the French people this morning. They seem to think the pilot was a man called Condré – Jules Condré.

TEMPLE: (*Significantly*) Yes …

FORBES: (*Rather surprised*) Oh. Oh, I take it you've heard of Condré.

TEMPLE: Yes – I've heard of him, Sir Graham. (*Quietly*) I'll talk to you this afternoon.

FORBES: Yes, all right. (*Suddenly*) Oh, I suppose you've seen the newspapers?

TEMPLE: No, I'm afraid I haven't.

FORBES: They've splashed the Kelvin story right across the front page …

TEMPLE: (*Interested*) Oh … Oh, have they? What do they say?

FORBES: The usual nonsense! The Daily Post seems to think we've caught the bird we're looking for …

TEMPLE: Valentine?

FORBES: Yes … I wish I could think so …

TEMPLE: I take it you don't think Mr Kelvin is Valentine?

FORBES: Well, if he is – we can't prove it.

TEMPLE: Have you spoken to him?

FORBES: Yes – we had him up to the office this morning. He's changed, Temple.

TEMPLE: What do you mean?

FORBES: Oh – he's tougher; a little more full of himself.

TEMPLE: (*Interested*) Why, I wonder?

FORBES: I don't know. He didn't seem very sure of himself at half past two this morning, did he?

TEMPLE: He certainly did not!

FORBES: Anyway, you can see him for yourself, if you'd like to.

TEMPLE: That's quite an idea.

FORBES: All right! (*Closing the conversation*) Three o'clock!

TEMPLE: Three o'clock, Sir Graham – at Scotland Yard …

TEMPLE replaces the receiver.

FADE UP of MUSIC.

FADE DOWN of MUSIC.

As the music fades away, FADE UP of CHARLES KELVIN; the atmosphere is tense until KELVIN retires from the scene.

KELVIN: (*Irritated; but not by any means rattled*) … If I've told you once, I've told you a hundred times. I don't know anything at all about a man called Condras …

TEMPLE: (*With a note of authority*) Condré, Mr Kelvin! Condré.

KELVIN: Very well – Condré! I went down to Braysham to see someone called Layland; when I discovered that … (*He hesitates*)

TEMPLE: Yes?

KELVIN: … when I discovered that Mr Layland was not to be found there I … I decided to return to London.

TEMPLE: Is that why Superintendent Wetherby found you running away from the house?

KELVIN: (*Almost losing his temper*) I've told you! Sir Gilbert Dryden told me that Mr Layland was at the house, that's – that's the only reason why I went there.

TEMPLE: (*Not believing a word, and conveying this impression*) Oh … Oh, yes, of course!

KELVIN: (*Flaring up*) Don't you believe me?

TEMPLE: Do you expect me to believe you, Mr Kelvin?

KELVIN: (*Angry*) It's a matter of complete indifference to me whether you believe me or not!

171

TEMPLE:	Indeed? Very good, Mr Kelvin! (*Quietly, dismissing KELVIN*) All right, Sergeant!
FORBES:	(*Abruptly*) Take Mr Kelvin down to Superintendent Bradley's office.
SERGEANT:	Very good, sir! (*To KELVIN*) This way, please, sir …

The door opens, and closes.

With KELVIN's exit the atmosphere is much easier.

WETHERBY:	Ah! Well, you didn't get much change out of that young man, Mr Temple!
TEMPLE:	(*Thoughtfully*) No …
PETERS:	You know, in spite of Sheila Baxter's story about Sir Gilbert Dryden, I've still got a hunch about Kelvin.
FORBES:	What do you mean?
PETERS:	Well, I shouldn't be at all surprised if he doesn't turn out to be Valentine after all.
FORBES:	What makes you say that, Peters?
PETERS:	Well – we know he's mixed up in this business – that's obvious – and yet …
WETHERBY:	And yet when you get down to brass tacks we've got absolutely nothing on the boy.
PETERS:	Exactly!
FORBES:	Oh – I wouldn't go so far as to say that, Peters. Don't forget the Charlie King affair – he hasn't really given us a satisfactory explanation about the watch chain.
TEMPLE:	No, and I don't think he will either, Sir Graham.
FORBES:	Why?
TEMPLE:	Because in my opinion he murdered Charlie King …
WETHERBY:	(*Rather surprised*) Oh!
FORBES:	Does that mean?

172

PETERS: Well, that's a change anyway, Temple – we don't often find ourselves in agreement with each other.

TEMPLE: (*Quietly, interested*) Peters, tell me – what exactly is your opinion about this Valentine affair?

PETERS: Well, to be quite frank, my opinion has changed quite a lot – especially during the past two or three days. When I first started investigating this business, I was under the impression that the whole affair was run, organised and completely controlled by one person – Valentine. (*Thoughtfully*) Now, however, I'm not so sure.

WETHERBY: (*Faintly irritated*) Whichever way you look at it, it simply boils down to the fact that we're up against a definite criminal organisation – an organisation on quite an unprecedented scale.

TEMPLE: That sounds exactly like a line out of one of my novels, Superintendent!

FORBES laughs.

PETERS: Well – what's your opinion, Temple?

TEMPLE: Well, Peters – I'll tell you. It's my belief that there exists in or near London a central depot – a sort of clearing house, if you like. Whenever any drugs – narcotics – are smuggled into the country, they eventually find their way to this central depot. At this depot, contact is made, and the drugs are eventually distributed all over the country. Now you know, Sir Graham – we all know from past experience – that it's a great mistake to assume that the drug habit exists only in a certain section of the community. A

173

drug addict isn't necessarily a wealthy person
…

PETERS: (*Interrupting TEMPLE*) But he must be wealthy, Temple – otherwise he'd never be able to buy the stuff!

TEMPLE: But that's the point! He doesn't always buy it!

FORBES: (*Sharply*) What do you mean?

TEMPLE: Sometimes it's given to him – for services rendered.

PETERS: (*Comprehending*) Oh …

WETHERBY: Now I see what you're getting at!

FORBES: You mean that the whole of the organisation is controlled by about three or four people – the petty, unimportant, but risky little jobs are undertaken by outsiders – drug addicts – people who would risk anything in order to satisfy their craving …

TEMPLE: Precisely …

PETERS: (*Slowly*) You mean, people like the man who impersonated the doctor, like the girl who impersonated the nurse …

TEMPLE: Exactly, Peters.

PETERS: Well, in that case how does Valentine fit into the picture?

FORBES: Quite easily, Peters! Valentine is the mysterious man behind the scenes. The big noise! The mysterious hand that …

TEMPLE: (*Quietly*) Oh, no! No, I don't think so, Sir Graham.

FORBES: (*A moment*) What do you mean?

TEMPLE: I think that's the extraordinary part about this affair. I don't think Valentine is the mysterious man behind the scenes, certainly not so far as the other people are concerned.

174

WETHERBY: You mean that the identity of Valentine is actually known to the other members of the organisation?

TEMPLE: Yes. Yes, I'm pretty sure it is, Wetherby.

FORBES: (*After a moment*) Temple, what do you think happened down at Braysham?

TEMPLE: Well, your guess is as good as mine, Sir Graham, but – if you want my opinion … Dryden contacted Layland and offered him three hundred and fifty pounds to go down to Braysham and collect a parcel from the pilot of a plane, a man called Jules Condré. When I picked up Layland at the San Chow restaurant, Dryden realised that something was the matter, wirelessed Condré, and told him to turn up at Braysham an hour or so earlier than was originally planned. Condré did this and waited for Layland.

FORBES: Go on …

TEMPLE: Now, this is the interesting point. In my opinion, Dryden intended that Condré should beat up Layland and then depart for the house – St Nicholas. At the house, it was intended that he should hand over the package to Charles Kelvin.

FORBES: Yes …

TEMPLE: But when Layland spoke to Condré, he impersonated O'Hara – now it's my opinion that Dryden hasn't said anything about this to Condré. This made Condré think. He came to the conclusion – quite correctly – that his friend O'Hara had been done away with and that if he turned up at the house …

175

FORBES: That fire! It must have been prepared for Condré …

TEMPLE: Exactly! Condré changed his plan – probably stayed the night on the sand dunes – and this morning …

FORBES: Telephoned Sir Gilbert!

WETHERBY: Yes!

PETERS: (*Excitedly*) It fits together all right, Temple. It fits together like a jigsaw, but …

FORBES: It points to Dryden! …

PETERS: Yes!

WETHERBY: Well – if Dryden does turn up tonight – if Dryden meets Condré – then by George he's Valentine and you'll never convince me otherwise. Sir Graham!

FORBES: I shan't try, Wetherby, don't worry about that!

PETERS: I say, this business is going to mess your evening up, isn't it, Wetherby?

WETHERBY: Can't be helped.

TEMPLE: Had you other plans for this evening?

WETHERBY: It's my daughter. She's making her debut tonight, as you might say. She's in the new play at the Queens. First time she's been in the West End.

TEMPLE: Oh. Oh, well, I hope she'll have a big success, Wetherby.

WETHERBY: Thank you.

TEMPLE: If it's a dramatic part, I feel sure she'll – er – ring the bell.

WETHERBY: (*Clearing his throat*) Er – yes, sir.

The door opens.

FORBES: (*Briskly*) What is it, Sergeant?

SERGEANT: I've been through to O Division, sir – all arrangements are complete for this evening.

FORBES: Good!
WETHERBY: You've notified Harper and the Flying Squad
             people?
SERGEANT: Yes, sir.
FORBES: All right, Sergeant!
SERGEANT: Thank you, sir.
The door closes.
FORBES: Well ...
PETERS: (*After a moment*) This is it ...
WETHERBY: Yes ...
FORBES: I'll pick you up at six o'clock, Temple ...
FADE UP of MUSIC.

FADE DOWN of MUSIC.
*FADE UP of traffic noises and background of Piccadilly
Circus.*
FADE UP of a police car patrolling down Regent Street.
TEMPLE, FORBES and a SERGEANT (driving) are in the car.
FORBES: What time do you make it, Temple?
TEMPLE: It's nearly ten to seven.
FORBES: (*Rather worried*) I think I'd contact Rogers
             again, Sergeant.
SERGEANT: Yes, sir.
FORBES: I don't know why, but I feel as nervous as a
             kitten! I hope there aren't going to be any slip-
             ups, Temple!
TEMPLE: I don't see why there should be. You've got a
             man watching each entrance to the tube, I take
             it?
FORBES: Yes ... Yes ... I'm not worried about that side
             of it. Once he gets inside the cordon, he'll
             never get out again ...
TEMPLE: Where's Wetherby?

FORBES: He's at the top – near the first escalator … as a
            matter of fact, he's collecting the tickets.
TEMPLE: And Peters?
FORBES: Peters is on the look-out for Condré – he's
            actually on the platform …
TEMPLE: Good …

FADE UP of oscillation, whistling, etc from a transmitter-
radio. The oscillation stops and we hear ROGERS.

ROGERS: Calling KCD 842 … Calling KCD 842 …
            Calling KCD 842 …
SERGEANT: (*Click; switch-over*) KCD 842 reporting!
            Contact! Over to you! (*Switch-over*)
ROGERS: A man answering to the description of Sir
            Gilbert Dryden left the house in Berkeley
            Square just over six minutes ago. I will repeat
            that. A man answering to the description of Sir
            Gilbert Dryden left the house in Berkeley
            Square just over six minutes ago. (*Click*)
FORBES: (*Quickly*) What's he dressed in, Rogers?
            (*Click*)
ROGERS: He's dressed in a blue suit, dark overcoat, black
            homburg hat, and he's carrying a light brown
            valise. I will repeat that. He's dressed in …
            (*His voice continues during FORBES' speech*)
FORBES: (*Quickly*) That's Dryden all right!
TEMPLE: Yes!
FORBES: He's on his way!!!! O.K. Sergeant!
SERGEANT: (*Switching ROGERS off*) O.K. Rogers! Report
            back to headquarters!

Quick FADE UP of MUSIC.

FADE DOWN of MUSIC.

FADE UP noises of the large entrance hall of Piccadilly Tube Station. People buying tickets. Sound of escalators. Ticket machines, etc.

FADE UP of an escalator and WETHERBY.

WETHERBY: Tickets please ... Thank you ... (*He clips tickets*) ... Tickets please ...

LADY: Do I change for Euston?

WETHERBY: Er – No. Straight through ... Tickets please ... (*He continues clipping tickets*)

A pause.

FORBES: (*Quietly*) Where's Peters – on the platform?

WETHERBY: Yes ...

FORBES: Dryden should be here any minute now ... He left the house about ten minutes ago.

WETHERBY: (*Quietly*) Good ...

TEMPLE: You've told Peters to do nothing until he actually contacts Condré?

FORBES: Yes ...

WETHERBY: Tickets, please ... Tickets, please ...

TEMPLE: (*Amused*) You make a very good ticket collector, Wetherby ...

WETHERBY: I'm glad you think so, Mr Temple ...

FORBES: (*Quickly*) Isn't that Dryden?!

TEMPLE: Where?!

FORBES: Over on the other side – near that machine!

TEMPLE: Yes! Yes, that's him!

FORBES: O.K. – get down to the platform, Temple, and warn Peters!

TEMPLE: Watch these stairs, if he makes a dash for it, he might try and get back this way!

FORBES: It'll be just the same if he does – there's a man on every exit!

FADE UP noise of the escalator.

FADE DOWN and CROSS FADE to the noise of a crowded platform.

PETERS: (*Quietly; surprised*) Oh, hello, Temple!

TEMPLE: (*Casually; but significantly casual*) Hello, Peters. He's on his way down …

PETERS: Oh. O.K. …

TEMPLE: Have you seen Condré?

PETERS: Well, I've seen the man I think is Condré. He's at the other end of the platform.

TEMPLE: Is there anyone down there?

PETERS: Yes – Crane and Bradley …

TEMPLE: It's a great pity there are so many people on the platform, if by any …

PETERS: (*Quickly*) Here's the fellow I mean … strolling up the platform … the chap with the attaché case …

TEMPLE: Yes … Yes, I think you're right … that could be Condré …

PETERS: He's perhaps a little younger than I imagined he would be …

TEMPLE: (*Quickly; tensely*) Here's Dryden!!!!

PETERS: (*Almost a whisper; tensely*) O.K. …

TEMPLE: (*Quietly; a warning*) Now watch him …

FADE UP slightly of platform chatter.

FADE DOWN again.

DRYDEN: (*Seriously; faintly ill at ease*) Monsieur Condré?

CONDRÉ: (*On guard; a Frenchman of about forty*) Oui …

DRYDEN: My name is Dryden …

CONDRÉ: Ah, yes! … Sir Gilbert! Good evening, sir!

DRYDEN: Have you got the …

CONDRÉ: (*Interrupting DRYDEN*) It is here … in the case …

DRYDEN: Why didn't you go to the house in Braysham?

CONDRÉ: Don't you know why I didn't go to the house, my friend?

180

DRYDEN: (*Annoyed*) Now listen, Condré! The next time you receive instructions from …

CONDRÉ: (*Flaring up*) Instructions! I don't receive instructions from anyone, my friend, not even from you! So, if you don't … (*He stops; a complete change of manner*) Who … is … this … man?

DRYDEN: (*Turning; quickly*) Where?

PETERS: (*In an official manner*) Sir Gilbert Dryden?

DRYDEN: Yes …

PETERS: My name is Peters – Major Peters of the C.I.D. This is Superintendent Bradley and Inspector Crane. We have a warrant for your arrest …

CONDRÉ: (*Suddenly; violently*) Don't move! Stand back! Don't move – any of you!!! (*There is a sudden stir amongst the people on the platform. One or two voices are heard*)

1st PERSON: What's happening?

2nd PERSON: Oh, dear, what's the matter?

3rd PERSON: He's got a revolver!

4th PERSON: Oh! He's got a revolver!

TEMPLE: (*Quickly*) Watch Dryden, Peters! Don't let him get away!!!

On the other platform, a train is approaching and during the following scene, the train arrives at the platform, the doors are opened, and the passengers leave the train.

CONDRÉ: Stand back! If anyone moves by God I'll let him have it!!!

BRADLEY: (*Worried*) Watch him, Mr Temple – he's desperate!

TEMPLE: Condré, listen!!! Don't be a fool …

A girl screams; there is a general nervous, frightened movement amongst the people on the platform. They are just starting to panic.

181

CONDRÉ: (*Desperately*) Don't come near me! D'you hear
               that? Don't come near me!!!

*CONDRÉ swears in French and fires the revolver. There is a
wild gasp from the crowd; they start to panic.*

TEMPLE: (*Angrily*) You fool!!! You stupid ... damn ...
               fool!!! (*He throws himself at CONDRÉ*)

CONDRÉ: (*Struggling*) Take your hands off me! Take
               your hands off me!!!! Take your hands off me
               you swine!!!!

A sudden gasp from the crowd.

BRADLEY: Look out, sir, he's falling off the platform!!!!

*CONDRÉ gives a quick, terrified gasp as he falls: a sudden
wild scream from a girl on the platform; the crowd surge
together completely out of control.*

TEMPLE: Don't panic!!!! (*Shouting above the excited
               voices*) Don't panic!!!!

BRADLEY: (*Shouting*) Keep still!!!! For heavens sake keep
               still!!!!

PETERS: (*Desperately*) Where's Dryden? Where's
               Dryden?!!!!

TEMPLE: (*Quickly*) I thought he was with you!

PETERS: He was! I was standing next to him – I was
               holding his arm – when suddenly ...

BRADLEY: (*A quick shout*) There he is!!! He's trying to get
               through onto the other platform!!!

PETERS: Oh, my God!

TEMPLE: (*Fighting his way through the crowd*) Be
               quick!!! Be quick, Bradley!!!!

PETERS: (*Wildly*) Stop him, Bradley!!!! Don't let him
               get on the train!!!!

TEMPLE: (*Still fighting his way through the excited
               crowd*) Out of the way ... Out of the bl ... Be
               quick!!! Be quick, Bradley!!!

FADE UP the noise of the other platform. The train is almost ready to leave.

GUARD: Stand clear of the gates! Stand clear everybody!!!! Stand clear!!!!

TEMPLE: There he is!!!!

PETERS: There he is, Bradley!!!!

TEMPLE: Be quick!!!!

The bell is heard. The gates close. The train commences to move.

TEMPLE: (*Breathlessly*) My God, he's made it!!!

The train gathers speed.

TEMPLE: He's made it, Peters!!!! He's on the train!!!!

PETERS, TEMPLE and BRADLEY are exhausted.

FADE UP of the train making a speedy departure. The noise of the train continues for a little while and then fades away.

FADE UP of MUSIC.

FADE DOWN of MUSIC.

FADE UP of SIR GRAHAM FORBES rattling a telephone receiver.

FORBES: (*On the telephone; tremendously keyed up*) Hello! Hel … Listen! This is Forbes speaking! I've just received your message! I don't give two hoots what the security people say! I want a special announcement and I want it NOW!!!!

Quick FADE UP of MUSIC.

Quick FADE DOWN of MUSIC.

BBC ANNOUNCER: We interrupt our programmes this evening to bring you a special announcement from Sir Graham Forbes, Chief Commissioner of Police, New Scotland Yard. Listeners in the London area are requested to be on the lookout for Sir Gilbert Dryden, believed to be the notorious Valentine,

    leader of the mysterious criminal organisation which
    during the past few months … (*FADE*).
Quick FADE UP of MUSIC.

FADE DOWN of MUSIC.
Sound of a flat buzzer.
A door opens.
TEMPLE: (*Rather tired*) Hello, Mary …
MARY: Good evening, sir.
TEMPLE: Is Mrs Temple in?
MARY: Yes, sir. She got back from Evesham about an
    hour ago …
TEMPLE: Oh, good!
MARY: You'll find her in the lounge, sir, with Miss Baxter.
TEMPLE: Oh. Oh, thank you, Mary …
The lounge door opens and closes.
STEVE: Oh, hello, Paul!
TEMPLE: Hello, darling! Hello, Miss Baxter!
STEVE: (*Quickly*) What happened?
SHEILA: What happened tonight at …
TEMPLE: He escaped … Oh, it was one hell of a mix-up!
STEVE: There's been an announcement about Dryden on the
    radio – they interrupted the programme.
TEMPLE: Yes, I know.
STEVE: What's going to happen?
TEMPLE: They're watching every Tube station in Town, but
    I've still got a hunch he'll get away with it!
STEVE: You look done in.
TEMPLE: Well – it hasn't exactly been a picnic.
STEVE: What does Sir Graham think about …
TEMPLE: Sir Graham! Oh – don't mention Sir Graham! Poor
    old Peters – he's certainly in hot water!
SHEILA: But what happened exactly?

TEMPLE: Condré made a dash for it – pulled a gun – and then we had just one beautiful panic! During the excitement, Dryden slipped onto the next platform and … jumped … onto a train.

SHEILA: (*Quickly, without thinking*) But couldn't you have stopped the train, Mr Temple?

TEMPLE: Well – I could have thrown an atomic bomb at it, I suppose, but …

SHEILA: I'm sorry …

TEMPLE: (*Pleasantly*) That's all right …

SHEILA: Well, I suppose I'd better be going …

TEMPLE: No … No, don't go … Not yet, Miss Baxter …

STEVE: Here we are, darling, here's a drink.

TEMPLE: Thanks. (*He drinks*) Ah, that's better! (*Brighter*) I'm glad you're here, Miss Baxter – I wanted to have a word with you.

SHEILA: I really don't know why I came here, Mr Temple! I was so jumpy and nervous and terribly on edge – I just couldn't sit still. I knew, of course, after what I told you this morning, that you'd try and arrest Sir Gilbert, but …

TEMPLE: You took it for granted that we should succeed? I wish we had, Miss Baxter – (*Seriously*) If only for your sake.

SHEILA: (*After a moment; seriously*) What do you mean?

STEVE: What do you mean, darling?

TEMPLE: I don't want to frighten you, Miss Baxter, but it's my belief that until Sir Gilbert Dryden is arrested, you're in rather an unfortunate position.

SHEILA: Why? Why do you say that?

TEMPLE: Because Dryden isn't a fool – not by any stretch of the imagination. He realises by now that someone discovered his arrangements – his arrangements to meet Condré – and went straight to Scotland Yard.

185

He'll remember that telephone call this morning, and ... he'll ... remember ...

SHEILA: (*Quickly; nervously*) Leaving me alone in the study ...?

TEMPLE: Yes.

STEVE: Paul – Paul, do you think he's dangerous? Do you think he'll make an attempt to ... (*She stops*)

Pause.

SHEILA: (*Nervously; almost a challenge*) Well? You know what Mrs Temple was going to say?

TEMPLE: (*Slowly*) I think you've got to watch yourself, Miss Baxter ...

SHEILA: (*A moment; then breaking the spell with a nervous laugh*) I shall sleep with my door locked and a very large hammer underneath my pillow.

STEVE: (*Laughing*) Where do you live, Miss Baxter?

SHEILA: I've a flat – well, I suppose you'd call it a maisonette – in Kenilworth Mansions, just off Park Lane ...

STEVE: Oh, yes ...

TEMPLE: Well, come along! We'll take you home – and give it the once over!

SHEILA: (*Laughing*) Oh, really there's no need to put ... (*She is interrupted by the telephone*)

TEMPLE: Excuse me. (*He lifts the receiver. On the phone*) Hello?

FORBES: Hello? Temple?

TEMPLE: Oh, hello, Sir Graham!

FORBES: (*Quietly; confidentially*) I'm sorry to disturb you – but I thought you'd like to know that I've – er – attended to that little matter.

TEMPLE: Oh! Oh, have you?

FORBES: It's quite settled. Quite definitely.

TEMPLE: Good. (*A moment*) Tonight?

FORBES: Yes, tonight …

TEMPLE: (*Suddenly; brightly*) Oh – well – thanks for ringing, Sir Graham!

FORBES: That's all right. Goodbye!

TEMPLE: Goodbye! (*He replaces the receiver*)

STEVE: That sounds very mysterious, darling?

TEMPLE: Well – (*He hesitates*) – I suppose I oughtn't to tell you this really, but – they've released Charles Kelvin.

SHEILA: Oh, I'm glad!

STEVE: Yes, so am I! I never really thought that he was mixed up in this business, and …

TEMPLE: He's mixed up in it all right – but unfortunately, we can't prove anything! Still, he isn't Valentine, we do know that. (*A sudden thought; to himself*) Or do we? (*Suddenly; back to normal*) Ah, well! Come along, Miss Baxter!

FADE UP of MUSIC.

FADE DOWN of MUSIC.

FADE UP of a key being taken out of a lock and the opening of a door.

SHEILA: Well – here we are!

STEVE: Oh, isn't it charming! Isn't it a lovely flat, Paul?

The door closes.

TEMPLE: Precisely what I expected.

SHEILA: (*Laughing*) Now – I wonder how I'm supposed to take that!

STEVE: (*Moving across the room*) Oh, I say – this is the dining room over here, and …

SHEILA: It's quite small. There's just the two rooms – lounge and dining room and two bedrooms upstairs.

TEMPLE: Miss Baxter, has Sir Gilbert ever been here?

SHEILA:	No. No, I don't think he has. He must know that I live here though because he telephoned …
STEVE:	(*Quietly*) What is it?
SHEILA:	Why – why, there's someone upstairs!
TEMPLE:	Are you sure?
SHEILA:	Listen!

A moment; someone can be heard moving about on the floor above.

TEMPLE:	Have you a maid or …
SHEILA:	Yes, I have a maid but she's away ill – she's been away for two weeks …
TEMPLE:	(*After a pause; quietly*) Where's the staircase?
SHEILA:	It's through the door over … (*Quickly, nervously*) Mr Temple – Mr Temple, do you think it's Sir Gilbert, because …
STEVE:	(*Tensely*) Well, whoever it is, they're coming downstairs …
TEMPLE:	(*Softly*) Yes! Now don't move, Miss Baxter – stay where you are …
STEVE:	But Paul …
TEMPLE:	Stand still, darling!

A long pause.
The door opens.
STEVE gives a quick gasp of surprise.

WETHERBY:	(*Surprised; but quite pleasantly*) Oh, hello, Mr Temple! I didn't expect to find you here, sir!
TEMPLE:	(*Surprised, but faintly amused*) Well, if it comes to that, I didn't expect to find you here either, Superintendent …

FADE UP of MUSIC.

END OF EPISODE SEVEN

EPISODE EIGHT

IN WHICH PAUL TEMPLE
MEETS VALENTINE

OPEN TO:

STEVE: (*Quietly*) What is it?

SHEILA: Why – why, there's someone upstairs!

TEMPLE: Are you sure?

SHEILA: Listen!

A moment; someone can be heard moving about on the floor above.

TEMPLE: Have you a maid or …

SHEILA: Yes, I have a maid but she's away ill – she's been away for two weeks …

TEMPLE: (*After a pause; quietly*) Where's the staircase?

SHEILA: It's through the door over … (*Quickly, nervously*) Mr Temple – Mr Temple, do you think it's Sir Gilbert, because …

STEVE: (*Tensely*) Well, whoever it is, they're coming downstairs …

TEMPLE: (*Softly*) Yes! Now don't move, Miss Baxter – stay where you are …

STEVE: But Paul …

TEMPLE: Stand still, darling!

A long pause.

The door opens.

STEVE gives a quick gasp of surprise.

WETHERBY: (*Surprised; but quite pleasantly*) Oh, hello, Mr Temple! I didn't expect to find you here, sir!

TEMPLE: (*Surprised, but faintly amused*) Well, if it comes to that, I didn't expect to find you here either, Superintendent …

WETHERBY: (*Suddenly, a little laugh*) No … No, I don't expect you did, sir! Although, I bet a fiver, we're both here for the same reason.

TEMPLE: (*Quietly*) What is your reason, Wetherby?

WETHERBY: Well, sir – I figured it out this way. In view of what's happened tonight, Sir Gilbert Dryden isn't going to feel particularly friendly towards Miss Baxter. It's my bet that he'll turn up here and …

TEMPLE: (*Interrupting WETHERBY*) Oh! Oh, and you wanted to make certain that …

WETHERBY: That he hasn't already done so! Exactly! He might have made a beeline for this place.

SHEILA: Oh!

WETHERBY: Oh, it's all right, Miss – the flat's quite empty. You've nothing to worry about.

SHEILA: (*Nervously*) Well – I – I don't know about that! You're all making me feel particularly nervous, I …

STEVE: Miss Baxter, why don't you collect a few things and spend the night with us? We've got a spare room …

TEMPLE: That's an awfully good idea, Steve! Now why on earth didn't we think of that before?

SHEILA: (*A little laugh*) No, really … it was silly of me … I'll be all right. In any case, if I don't want to stay here, I can always go to a friend of mine at …

The telephone interrupts SHEILA.

WETHERBY: (*After a moment*) Who's that?

SHEILA: I haven't the faintest idea!

WETHERBY: I'll take it!

TEMPLE: No! No, let Miss Baxter take it …

The receiver is lifted.

SHEILA: (*On the phone*) Hello? (*Puzzled*) Yes … Yes … Yes … (*Impatiently*) Yes, I've told you this is Grosvenor 7296! (*Aside to TEMPLE*) I haven't the vaguest idea who it is! (*On the phone*) What? (*Suddenly*) Who is that? … Who? … (*Quickly, frightened*) Oh! Sir Gilbert!!!

192

TEMPLE:	(*Quickly*) Here … let me have it! … Quickly! (*He takes the phone*) Listen, Dryden, if you've got any sense … Damn!!!!
WETHERBY:	(*Quickly*) What's happened?
TEMPLE:	(*Quietly*) He's rung off … (*He replaces the receiver*)
STEVE:	Did he say anything?
TEMPLE:	(*Thoughtfully*) He … No, he must have heard my voice when I took the phone from Miss Baxter …
WETHERBY:	I wonder if you can trace the call?
SHEILA:	He was in a callbox, I heard him press the button …
WETHERBY:	(*Disappointed*) Oh …
TEMPLE:	(*Quickly, tensely*) What did he say? What did he say exactly?
SHEILA:	(*Bewildered*) Well, I – I don't really know what he said. I couldn't understand him at first – in fact, I didn't even recognise him.
WETHERBY:	What do you mean?
SHEILA:	Well, to be quite honest, he sounded to me almost as if – well – as if he was drunk!
TEMPLE:	But he must have said something!
SHEILA:	Well, when I picked the phone up, he said is that Grosvenor 7296 and I said yes … and then he said is that Grosvenor 7296 again … and I said yes, and then for the life of me I don't know why – but … he repeated the question. You know, I'm sure he was drunk!
TEMPLE:	Go on – and then what did he say?
SHEILA:	Well, then – when I asked him who it was, he said: "Sheila, this … *(She is obviously distressed now and losing her nerve)* … is Gilbert" … (*She is near to tears*)

193

TEMPLE: (*Quietly*) Thanks. Now don't get upset, Miss Baxter.

STEVE: Come along; I think you'd better come back to the flat with us …

SHEILA: (*Pulling herself together*) No! No … I'm staying here. I shall be perfectly all right – it's silly of me to get like this. I'm – I'm terribly sorry.

TEMPLE: Are you sure you'll be all right?

SHEILA: Yes – yes, honestly. I'm not a bit nervous now … really, I'm not …

TEMPLE: Well, if you say so, Miss Baxter! Come along, Steve! You've got my number just in case …

SHEILA: Yes – yes, I've got your number – and thanks for everything.

STEVE: (*A little laugh*) Nonsense, my dear!

TEMPLE: Ready, Superintendent?

WETHERBY: Yes, I'm ready, sir. Now you've no need to worry, Miss Baxter. I'm planting one of my best men outside on the landing. He'll be there all night – if he hears any funny business, he'll be in here like a streak of lighting!

SHEILA: (*Relieved; laughing*) Oh, thank you, Superintendent!

WETHERBY: So you've nothing to worry about! (*With a laugh*) This Valentine guy might be pretty smart but he's not exactly the invisible man, is he, Mr Temple?

TEMPLE: Not … exactly … Superintendent. (*Pleasantly*) Goodnight, Miss Baxter!

SHEILA: Goodnight!

A door opens.

SHEILA: Goodnight, Mrs Temple!

STEVE: Goodnight!

SHEILA: Goodnight, Superintendent!

WETHERBY: Goodnight, Miss.

The door closes.

WETHERBY: Ah! Ah, here you are, Sergeant!

HODSON: (*A cockney, but not too broad*) Evening, sir! Superintendent Bradley told me to report …

WETHERBY: Yes! Yes, that's right, Sergeant! (*Aside*) I shan't keep you a moment, Mr Temple!

TEMPLE: That's all right, Wetherby!

WETHERBY: Now, Sergeant, listen! This is Miss Baxter's flat – Flat B17. Now, I don't know whether Superintendent Bradley …

HODSON: The Superintendent gave me my instructions, sir.

WETHERBY: Oh, good!

HODSON: (*Not too happy*) I take it it's an all-night job, sir?

WETHERBY: (*Sympathetically*) Yes, I'm afraid it is, Hodson.

HODSON: M'm – very good, sir.

WETHERBY: I'll try and get some sandwiches sent up to you – there's a service restaurant on the ground floor.

HODSON: Oh – I'd be obliged if you would, sir.

WETHERBY: Yes, all right, Sergeant. Goodnight!

HODSON: Goodnight, sir!

WETHERBY: (*Briskly*) I'm ready, Mr Temple!

The lift gates close. Start the sound of the lift.

FADE SCENE.

FADE UP of the lift.

The lift stops and the gate opens.

ALICE: (*Rather a saucy type*) Are you the gentleman Superintendent Wetherby ordered the sandwiches for?

HODSON: That's right – Sergeant Hodson!

ALICE: Well, here we are – don't make a beast of yourself!

HODSON: Ooo! What d'you call this – mustard and cress?

ALICE: No, chicken …

HODSON: Oh!

ALICE: … paste …

HODSON: Oh!

ALICE: What are you doing up here on the landing anyway?

HODSON: Haven't they told you? We're expecting a murder!

ALICE: (*Taking HODSON seriously*) A murder!

HODSON: S'right! Cock-robin …

ALICE: (*Nearly taken in*) … Cock-robin … Sauce!!!!

HODSON laughs.

The lift gate bangs.

FADE DOWN of the lift.

HODSON:(*To himself; munching a sandwich*) Chicken! Blimey, if this is chicken – then I'm a ham!

Suddenly, a noise is heard coming from SHEILA's flat. A man's voice can be heard raised in anger – SHEILA is screaming. The man stops talking and SHEILA can be heard shouting for HODSON. She is desperately frightened.

SHEILA: Leave me alone! Don't touch me! Leave me alone!!! For God's sake … Help!!! Help!!!

HODSON: (*Springing to life; dropping his plate*) Strewth!!!

SHEILA: (*Nearly hysterical*) Help!!! Help!!! Don't touch me!!! Don't – don't touch me!!!

HODSON is banging on the door.

HODSON:Open up here!!! Open up!!! (*Forcing the door*) Get this … door … open …

SHEILA: Help!!! Please – please, help!!!

HODSON: (*Breaking the door in*) It's O.K., Miss Baxter … It's O.K. … (*He finally succeeds in breaking the door open*)

196

FADE UP of SHEILA BAXTER, frightened and exhausted.

SHEILA: He's – he's gone upstairs … be careful … be
               careful … he might … be … behind that door
               …

HODSON: Which door?

SHEILA: Over there! Be careful!!!

HODSON: Stand behind me, Miss Baxter!! (*Raising his
               voice*) Now, do you hear me? Come out!!!
               (*Fiercely*) D'you hear me, you swine!!! Come
               out!!! (*Slowly, a threat*) I'm going … to …
               open … the … door … and … if … you …
               don't … (*He suddenly throws open the door
               and there is a quick, immediate, revolver shot.
               HODSON gasps … and gasps again …*)

Quick FADE UP of MUSIC.

FADE DOWN of MUSIC.
FADE UP background noise of a large railway station.
CROSS FADE to:

STATION ANNOUNCER: The nine-fifteen for Middletown
               will leave from Platform 10, calling at
               Wendlesen, Dimborough, Radcliffe and
               Hurstford. Passengers for Radcliffe travel at the
               rear of the train. The nine-fifteen for
               Middletown will leave from Platform 10 –
               calling at Wendlesen, Dimborough, Radcliffe
               and Hurstford … (*FADE AWAY of voice*)

1st PORTER: (*In the left-luggage office*) I should put that
               case up on the top, Harry! That's it!

KELVIN: (*Quietly*) Good evening – is this the left
               luggage office?

1st PORTER: Well, it aint' the Palace o' Varieties, brother!

KELVIN: (*A little laugh*) Of course … how stupid!

1st PORTER: What can we do for you?

KELVIN: I – I left a case here about a week ago, a small brown case …

1st PORTER: Have you got the ticket?

KELVIN: (*Searching*) Yes, I … Ah, here we are!

1st PORTER: Ta … (*He whistles to himself, moves to the background amongst the cases*) What name?

KELVIN: (*Calling to the PORTER*) Kelvin!

1st PORTER: Here we are! (*Coming forward with a case*) Here we are, mate! That'll cost you …

KELVIN: (*Throwing a coin on to the counter*) Keep the change!

1st PORTER: (*Surprised*) Oh … Oh, thanks, China!

FADE AWAY of station noises.

CROSS FADE to the station entrance; a taxi drives up – the sound of a meter.

1st TAXI: (*A broad Scotsman*) Where to?

KELVIN: I want you to take me to The Esplanade Hotel.

1st TAXI: The Esplanade? Now let's see – that's just off Regent Street, isn't it?

KELVIN: That's right.

1st TAXI: O.K. …

The taxi door slams; the taxi drives away as a second taxi pulls up.

2nd TAXI: 'Ere! 'Ere! Just a minute, mate! Not so fast!

BRADLEY: (*With quiet authority*) I want you to follow that cab in front – don't lose sight of him! You understand?

2nd TAXI: 'Ere, just a minute, mate!!! Just a …

BRADLEY: (*Quietly, but with authority*) My name's Bradley … Superintendent Bradley, C.I.D.

2nd TAXI: (*Impressed*) Oh! Oh! Okedoke, chum! Okedoke! (*He revs up the taxi*)

FADE UP of MUSIC.

FADE DOWN of MUSIC.

A flat buzzer is heard. A door opens.

TEMPLE: Hello, Mary! Any messages?

MARY: Yes, sir. Sir Graham Forbes telephoned a few moments ago, sir … Oh, and Major Peters is here, sir – he's just arrived.

STEVE: (*A little surprised*) Major Peters?

MARY: Yes, ma'am …

TEMPLE: (*Quietly*) What did Sir Graham want?

MARY: (*Seriously*) He asked me to deliver a message to you, sir. He said it was very important.

TEMPLE: Yes?

MARY: (*Puzzled; repeating the message*) He said, tell Mr Temple, it looks as if it might be The Esplanade …

STEVE: (*Surprised*) The Esplanade? But that was the hotel we …

TEMPLE: (*Interrupting STEVE; briskly*) Right! Thank you, Mary!

MARY: Thank you, sir.

TEMPLE: Come along, darling – let's see what Peters wants.

The lounge door opens.

PETERS: Ah! Hello, Temple!

TEMPLE: Hello, Major! Sorry to have kept you waiting!

PETERS: Oh, that's … Oh, good evening, Mrs Temple!

STEVE: Good evening, Major.

TEMPLE: Would you like a drink?

PETERS: No … no … I don't think so, sir – not just at the moment. As a matter of fact, I just dropped in to show you this – I thought you might be interested.

TEMPLE: What is it?

PETERS: It's a report on Lefty Stoner, sir – it came through on the teleprinter from our Newcastle people.

199

STEVE: Lefty Stoner? Oh! Oh, that was the man who tried to force us over the bridge last night …

PETERS: Yes. (*A moment*) I – I think it's what you've been looking for …

TEMPLE: (*Interested*) Oh. Oh, is it?

PETERS: (*A little laugh*) Well – judge for yourself. (*He passes the report to TEMPLE*)

TEMPLE: (*After a moment*) Yes … Yes … I should think this is it, all right. I see he was with the Dee Electrical Company for seven years.

PETERS: Yes.

STEVE: (*Slowly*) That's a nasty scratch you've got, Major!

PETERS: H'm. (*Suddenly; a laugh*) Oh – Oh, yes! I had a choice, Mrs Temple – either a scratch or be pushed off the platform!

TEMPLE: It certainly was a scrimmage! (*PETERS laughs; then TEMPLE suddenly closes the conversation*) Right! Thank you, Peters!

PETERS: Goodnight, sir. Goodnight, Mrs Temple!

STEVE: Goodnight, Major.

PETERS: (*Briskly*) It's all right – it's all right, old boy! I can let myself out …

The door opens and closes.

STEVE: Well – what was all that about, darling?

TEMPLE: (*Faintly amused by STEVE's bewilderment*) You heard – it was about a man called Lefty Stoner. (*Suddenly*) No, don't take your things off, Steve, we're going out again.

STEVE: Out? Where?

TEMPLE: (*Quietly; after a tiny pause*) To … The Esplanade …

STEVE: (*Surprised*) The Esplanade! Paul, what did Sir Graham mean by that message? The message he …

200

TEMPLE: (*Interrupting STEVE; quickly*) Not now, darling! Come along! We haven't a moment to lose, we've got to …

STEVE: (*For the first time; a sudden, determined, note of authority*) Paul, please!!! (*A moment; quietly, seriously*) Darling – what's this all about?

TEMPLE: (*A pause; seriously*) You remember The Esplanade?

STEVE: Yes, of course, I remember it! It's the hotel where we had dinner the first night this business started, the night … (*Thoughtfully, remembering*) … the night that girl disappeared … the night we bumped into Superintendent Wetherby.

TEMPLE: (*Slowly*) Yes …

STEVE: (*Puzzled; serious and tense in manner*) But, Paul, why do you want to go to The Esplanade tonight … tonight of all nights …?

TEMPLE: Because …

STEVE: Well?

TEMPLE: Because I've got a hunch that … Valentine … is going … to … be … there …

STEVE: (*Astonished*) Valentine! But – but Sir Gilbert wouldn't turn up at a hotel, not when he realises that the whole of Scotland Yard are …

TEMPLE: (*Quietly; interrupting STEVE*) Not Sir Gilbert, darling … Valentine …

STEVE: (*Softly, amazed*) What do you mean? What do you mean???!!!

TEMPLE: (*Slowly*) I mean that Sir Gilbert Dryden isn't … Valentine …

STEVE: (*Aghast*) Isn't … Then – then who is it?? Paul! Paul, who is Valentine????

TEMPLE: Don't you know? (*A moment*) Don't you know, Steve?

FADE UP of MUSIC.

201

FADE DOWN of MUSIC.
FADE UP of a car. It draws slowly into the kerb.

STEVE: (*Puzzled*) What are you pulling up here for, darling? This isn't The Esplanade – The Esplanade's over on the corner near …

TEMPLE: Yes, Steve, I know … (*Suddenly, quietly*) Ah, here he is!

STEVE: Who is it?

TEMPLE: It's Sir Graham … (*The car door opens*) Hello, Sir Graham!

FORBES: (*Quietly; but tense in manner; the impression is almost that of a tense whisper*) Hello, Temple! You got my message all right then?

TEMPLE: Yes …

FORBES: Hello, Steve! I've got my car on the corner, Temple – I think I should come over there, if I were you – we can see the main entrance to the hotel.

TEMPLE: Yes, all right … Where's Wetherby?

FORBES: I let him go to his daughter's first night. It's a big occasion for him. Bradley's over on the other side watching the side entrance. He's with the Flying Squad people.

TEMPLE: Good!

FORBES: We're leaving nothing to chance this time, Temple!

The car door opens: TEMPLE and STEVE get out of the car.

FORBES: Come along, Steve …

FADE SCENE.

FADE UP footsteps. A car door opens.

FORBES: Jump in the back, Steve.

STEVE: Thank you …

TEMPLE, STEVE and SIR GRAHAM enter the car.

TEMPLE:　　The Kelvin hunch turned up trumps all right then?

FORBES:　　It looks like it. Bradley was on his tail from the moment he left us. Incidentally, it looks as if some of the drugs were parked in the left luggage office at Waterloo. Kelvin picked up a case there　about twenty minutes ago.

STEVE:　　(*Surprised*) Then Kelvin – Charles Kelvin is … Valentine!

FORBES:　　(*Quickly; having seen something*) Hello, what's that?? Who's that leaving the hotel?

TEMPLE:　　It's all right – it's not Kelvin …

STEVE:　　(*Bewildered*) But, Sir Graham, if you know that Charles Kelvin is Valentine, and you know that he's in that hotel …

The call sign is heard on the car radio.

FORBES:　　Just a minute, Steve!!!

FORBES switches on the radio.

BRADLEY:(*From the radio: quickly*) Calling Car KB789 … Calling CAR KB 789 … Calling CAR KB 789 … Calling Car …

FORBES:　　(*Switch over*) Hello, Bradley! Hello! Contact! (*Click*)

BRADLEY:(*Excitedly*) Sir Graham, there's a car just pulled up to the side entrance … I think this is it!!! (*Quickly*) Yes!!! Yes … yes … Yes, it's Kelvin! He's getting into the car!!

FORBES:　　(*Switch over*) Who's driving, Bradley? (*Click*)

BRADLEY:I can't see, sir, although it looks to me like … They're moving!!! They're coming round the block, sir!!!

FORBES:　　(*Switch over*) O.K.! Warn the Squad people, Bradley! (*He switches off the radio: grimly*) This is it, Temple!

TEMPLE:	Have they got to pass here?
FORBES:	Yes – Yes, they can't help it!
TEMPLE:	Get down, Steve! Get down in the bottom of the car!!!
STEVE:	But, Paul, surely …
TEMPLE:	Do as I tell you, darling!!! Have you got a revolver, Sir Graham?
FORBES:	Yes – here we are … What are you going for, the back tyre?
TEMPLE:	Yes, unless we have a chance to …

The sound of an approaching car.

FORBES:	Here's the car!!!

The car draws near, and then in the distance, behind the approaching car, we hear the Flying Squad.

FORBES:	Here's the car, Temple!!!
TEMPLE:	They've spotted us!!! Get down, Steve!!!

The car draws level and as it does so, there is the sharp, staccato noise of machine gun fire – from a tommy gun. The windscreen of FORBES' car smashes to pieces.

STEVE:	(*Desperately*) Darling, are you all right?
TEMPLE:	Yes!!! Now for it!!! (*He fires and there is the explosion of the burst tyre*)

STEVE screams: there is a tremendous crash as the car overturns … and overturns.

Quick FADE UP of the Flying Squad.

FADE SCENE.

Quick FADE UP of the car burning: cars driving up to the scene of the accident: people gathering.

STEVE:	(*Distressed*) Oh, Paul! Paul, what a terrible accident – what a terrible accident!
BRADLEY:	(*Briskly*) We've got Kelvin, sir!
FORBES:	Good.
TEMPLE:	Is he badly hurt?

BRADLEY: He's in a pretty bad way, Mr Temple.

TEMPLE: (*Quietly*) And … Valentine?

BRADLEY: (*A moment*) Valentine was lucky, sir, not so much as a scratch!

STEVE: (*Staggered*) Valentine! But – But I thought Charles Kelvin was Valentine …

TEMPLE: No, darling …

STEVE: But Paul! Who – is – Valentine?

BRADLEY: Come and see for yourself, Mrs Temple!

TEMPLE: (*Quietly*) Come along, darling …

They walk nearer the wreckage.

SERGEANT: (*Officious*) Excuse me, sir – you can't … Oh! Oh, I beg your pardon, Mr Temple! Keep back there! Keep back, please!

TEMPLE: (*After a pause*) There we are, Steve …

STEVE: (*Slowly; aghast*) Why – why it's … Sheila Baxter!!!

TEMPLE: Yes, darling – Sheila Baxter … alias … Valentine!

STEVE: Valentine!

SHEILA: You think you're smart, don't you, Mr Temple?

TEMPLE: Yes, I think so, Miss Baxter!

SHEILA: Well, I don't think you've been quite so smart as you imagine! In the first place, you can't prove anything, and if you could …

TEMPLE: Yes, Miss Baxter – if we could …?

SHEILA: If you could, do you think I'd let them take me? Do you think I'd let them take me alive? I'll see you in hell first!

FORBES: Watch her, Sergeant! Don't let her make a dash for it!

SHEILA: Mr Temple, you might get me to Scotland Yard, if you're lucky you might even get me to testify against certain …

FORBES: Watch her, Sergeant!!!!

SHEILA: Really, Superintendent, there's no need to be alarmed! It's only my cigarette holder I'm getting out of my bag. I take it there's no objection if I have a cigarette?

TEMPLE: There's every objection, Miss Baxter!

BRADLEY: You don't think we're falling for an old trick like that, do you?

SHEILA: An old trick? Oh, you thought the cigarette might be poisoned? Then may I have one of yours? You don't mind if I use my holder, although I see you don't entirely trust me, Superintendent!

FORBES: This isn't a case of trusting you, Miss Baxter – We want you alive!

SHEILA: Don't worry, if I decide to stand for trial …

BRADLEY: You'll stand for trial all right!

SHEILA: You think so, Superintendent? You think so?

STEVE: (*Suddenly*) Oh, Paul! Paul!!!

FORBES: What's happening to her?!

STEVE: Paul, she must have taken something?! She must have poisoned herself! She must have taken …

TEMPLE: It was in the cigarette holder! I ought to have guessed! That business about the cigarette was just a bluff.

FORBES: Bradley – contact the Emergency Squad. Tell them to get the Police Doctor!!!!

STEVE: What is it, Paul? Is she …?

TEMPLE: She's dead …

FADE UP of MUSIC.

Slow FADE DOWN of MUSIC.

TEMPLE, STEVE and SIR GRAHAM are in the flat sitting behind the fire; they are having tea.

TEMPLE: Another cup of tea, darling, please …

STEVE: Sir Graham?

FORBES: Not for me, thank you, Steve …

TEMPLE: (*Merrily eating away*) Have another scone …

STEVE: Paul, don't eat with your mouth full!

FORBES laughs.

TEMPLE: (*Still eating*) What you mean is don't talk with your …

STEVE: (*Laughing*) You know perfectly well what I mean!

TEMPLE: (*Laughing; a moment, then*) You know, Sir Graham – I think in many ways, this Valentine affair has been probably the most interesting case I've worked on. You see, from my point of view, it was interesting because – quite early on – I discovered that one had to examine this case without prejudice and with rather – rather …

FORBES: Rather an unconventional outlook?

TEMPLE: Exactly!

STEVE: What do you mean, darling?

TEMPLE: Well, I think I'm correct in saying that when Scotland Yard first heard about Valentine, they laboured under the impression that the organisation was a comparatively new one, and that – like the Rex, Lorraine, and Marquis organisations – it was controlled utterly and completely by one person, namely – Valentine. Now actually, of course, this was not the case. The organisation had been in existence for some considerable time and, when I was first introduced to the case, was actually undergoing certain rather – how can one put it – rather revolutionary changes. In short, Sir Gilbert

Dryden was endeavouring to force Sheila Baxter – or Valentine, if you like – out of the picture and …

STEVE: And gain control of the organisation himself!

TEMPLE: Exactly, Steve! You see, coupled with the fact that Sheila Baxter, Sir Gilbert Dryden and Charles Kelvin were working together – as far as the general activities of the organisation were concerned – we had also to contend with the fact that privately, Sir Gilbert was intent upon double-crossing Sheila and Sheila was intent on double-crossing Sir Gilbert. Now let me give you a perfect example of this. Dryden, Sheila Baxter, and Charles Kelvin discovered that I had visited Snooker Riley. They all discovered that Snooker and O'Hara – who incidentally were part of the organisation – were accordingly suspected of double-crossing them and were taken care of. Sir Gilbert, Sheila, and Kelvin all agreed that Kelvin should contact a certain Mr Layland and pay him to impersonate Captain O'Hara – this Captain O'Hara, in other words Layland – would send Steve and myself to Estonia Avenue and we would find the dead body of the real O'Hara.

FORBES: In other words, a nice friendly warning telling you to keep your nose out of their business!

TEMPLE: Precisely. But Charles Kelvin, at Sheila Baxter's suggestion, brought Sir Gilbert Dryden's name into the story – the story that Layland was paid to tell us during his O'Hara impersonation – and Sheila Baxter strengthened the story by placing the note addressed to Sir Gilbert on the mat at Estonia Avenue. Sir Gilbert, of course, knew nothing about this, he simply thought Layland had dished out the original story.

STEVE: But, darling, that night, the night Sheila Baxter was attacked downstairs near the lift, was that …

TEMPLE: It was Dryden. He had discovered by then that Sheila Baxter had taken a knife – bearing his fingerprints – and planted it by the dead body of Snooker Riley. In other words, he now knew that she was playing precisely the same double-crossing game as himself.

STEVE: But I don't quite see how Charles Kelvin fits into the picture.

TEMPLE: Don't you, Steve? Isn't it rather obvious? Kelvin and Sheila Baxter? Kelvin's wife may have been a drug addict, but I bet you a fiver that's not why she committed suicide. Incidentally, you remember that night – the night the revolver was planted in our bedroom …?

STEVE: Yes?

TEMPLE: Sheila Baxter told us that she'd overheard Snooker Riley make arrangements with Sir Gilbert about the revolver …

STEVE: Well?

TEMPLE: Snooker Riley never fixed the contraption up – not in a thousand years! He couldn't even open a tin of sardines without splitting the tin from end to end.

FORBES laughs.

TEMPLE: The revolver was planted, at Sheila Baxter's instructions, by a man called Stoner – Lefty Stoner. Suddenly, in order to get herself into our confidence and to throw further suspicion on to Sir Gilbert, Sheila changed her mind and … Well … you remember that telephone call … the very first one we received?

STEVE: Yes?

TEMPLE: Now … let's go back to Charles Kelvin …

FORBES: Oh, I meant to tell you, Temple; Wetherby discovered why Kelvin murdered Charlie King; apparently Charlie King had decided to take sides in the issue and was violently pro-Dryden.

TEMPLE: (*A little laugh*) Yes, I guessed that when I realised that Dryden was a fairly frequent visitor to the San Chow! Incidentally, Sir Gilbert discovered that Kelvin was playing in with Sheila – that's why he sent him down to the house at Braysham. He knew, after I picked Layland up at the San Chow, that there was a pretty good chance of something going wrong.

FORBES: Quite obviously, the whole business was coming to a head! But tell me, Temple – did Jules Condré, the Frenchman – did he telephone Sir Gilbert and make arrangements …

TEMPLE: Of course he didn't telephone Sir Gilbert! When Condré realised that his friend O'Hara – the real O'Hara – had been done away with, then he contacted the one person that, so far as he was concerned, really mattered – Valentine. Sheila made all the arrangements for Dryden to meet him and then double-crossed the pair of them!

STEVE: Well, I can understand you suspecting Sheila, darling – but I still don't quite see how she gave herself away!

TEMPLE: Don't you!

FORBES laughs.

STEVE: No … no, I don't! And don't look so pleased with yourself either – the pair of you!

FORBES: Well, you see, Steve – last night Sir Gilbert didn't actually escape.

STEVE: What?!

FORBES: Oh, he got away from Piccadilly all right, but Temple and I picked him up about a quarter of an hour later in Leicester Square.

STEVE: (*Staggered*) Well, I'm ... But what about that radio announcement?

FORBES: Yes – the – er – radio announcement! I got into pretty hot water over that, Steve!

TEMPLE: I'm afraid I persuaded Sir Graham to send the radio announcement out – just as I persuaded him to release Charles Kelvin. And you see what happened, Steve. Sheila Baxter was under the impression that Dryden had escaped ...

STEVE: But he must have escaped! He telephoned her!

TEMPLE: Oh, no he didn't! It was Kelvin that telephoned Sheila Baxter, darling. He telephoned her and told her to meet him at The Esplanade Hotel. As a cover up, she pretended it was Dryden ...

FORBES: You know, Wetherby suspected Sheila Baxter. He ...

TEMPLE: (*Laughing*) Yes, I know he did! He was searching her flat when we got there!

STEVE: (*Puzzled*) But what about Hodson, the Sergeant? The man Superintendent Wetherby left behind on the landing!

TEMPLE: He had to be got rid of – so far as Sheila Baxter was concerned.

STEVE: But you don't understand, darling! Hodson heard Dryden! He heard the two of them struggling in the flat, he heard ...

TEMPLE: We can only suppose he heard Sheila Baxter screaming her head off against a gramophone record – he broke the door down, dashed into the flat, and as soon as his back was turned ... she let him have it ...

211

STEVE: (*Horrified*) Oh! Oh, how horrible!!! (*She is upset*)

TEMPLE: (*Calming STEVE*) It's all right, darling …

FORBES: Don't get upset, Steve, it's – it's over – it's all over, my dear.

STEVE: Yes. Yes, all ri – … (*Suddenly; remembering*) But Paul! Paul! It isn't all over!

TEMPLE: What do you mean?

STEVE: That girl! That girl! Who was that girl? That girl that …

TEMPLE: Oh, the – er – the girl that completely disappeared?

STEVE: Yes.

TEMPLE: Do you remember what happened that night, darling?

STEVE: Of course I remember!

TEMPLE: Wetherby walked to the end of the mews and when he came back he said …

STEVE: He said: "Well, there's no one there, Mr Temple!"

TEMPLE: Yes – (*Faintly amused*) Yes, but I'm afraid she was there, Steve – she was there all the time and Wetherby …

STEVE: But if she was there Wetherby must have seen her!

TEMPLE: Of course he saw her! As a matter of fact …

FORBES: (*Quite calmly*) As a matter of fact, it was his daughter, Steve. He planted her in the car and then walked round to the hotel in order to …

STEVE: Planted – her – in – the – car?

TEMPLE: (*Laughing*) Yes – and by Timothy she put up a pretty good show!

FORBES: Well – we were determined to rouse your curiosity and interest in the case, Temple! After all, you seemed particularly indifferent about the whole business when Peters and I …

STEVE: Well!!!!

They all laugh.

212

TEMPLE: Well, never mind, darling! From now on, no more murders, just a nice quiet holiday.

FORBES: Are you going away?

TEMPLE: Yes – we're going down to Bramley Lodge first thing tomorrow morning. And I'm going to sit back with my feet on the mantelpiece and, as Sam Dodsworth would say, think of nothing more important than the temperature of the beer – if there is anything more important, Sir Graham!

FORBES: (*Laughing*) You lucky people! Ah, well – I must be off! I'm supposed to be catching the six-fifteen to Denford.

TEMPLE: Well – goodbye, Sir Graham. It's been grand seeing you again, and I sincerely hope that the next time we … (*He stops dead; interested*) Did you   say Denford?

FORBES: Yes. (*Curious*) Why?

TEMPLE: Well – it's only two miles from Bramley.

FORBES: (*Quiet; gently*) Is it? I didn't know that.

TEMPLE: What are you going down to Denford for?

FORBES: (*A moment: seriously*) You mean to say you haven't seen the papers?

TEMPLE: What do you mean?

FORBES: Well – it's a most extraordinary business, Temple. The local people are completely out of their depth. Apparently, about a fortnight ago, they pulled a man out of the river. His name was Shearer – Carl Shearer.

TEMPLE: (*Intrigued*) Go on …

FORBES: (*Very serious*) Well, apparently this man Shearer had a peculiar mark on his right arm.

TEMPLE: (*Intensely interested*) Yes – yes, go on …

FORBES: And by a remarkable coincidence it resembled …

STEVE: (*With a tremendous sigh*) Oh!!! (*Weakly*) By Timothy, this is where I came in!!!!
FADE UP of MUSIC.

THE END

Francis Durbridge – The Human Thriller Factory
by **Charles Hatton**

A writer who has achieved fame and international reputation by concentrating almost exclusively on serials for radio and television is something of a rarity in this or any other country.

This is the achievement of Francis Durbridge, former student of Birmingham University, whose formative years were spent in Birmingham, where his father was a prominent businessman. Since his mother died in 1949, however, he has not paid many visits to the city but he still has very happy memories of the Midlands.

Always a great admirer of the work of Edgar Wallace, Durbridge's first serial in the history of broadcasting, *Send for Paul Temple*, had a strong Wallace flavour. But Durbridge began to diverge from Wallace almost immediately, preferring to concentrate on quality of output in preference to quantity.

Unlike the Fleet Street maestro, he has never had to churn out a couple of serials simultaneously in order to satisfy his creditors. For some years, Durbridge has been under contract to supply BBC Television with serials and he generally allows about three months for the writing of each serial.

During that period he works as intensively as the director of a car factory launching a new model. He lives the life of a semi-recluse, and the serial absorbs practically all his waking hours. He attends only to business matters, and sees few people socially outside his own family.

Over the years his serials have shown a considerable change in story values. They are no longer mainly concerned with crime – more than one murder per serial is rare – and he likes to think of them as stories about people involved in a change of highly dramatic events.

His scripts differ from his nearest rivals in this field in that they are invariably more tightly woven, with unexpected twists in the story and a general atmosphere of tensity that is achieved only by extremely intensive application on the part of the writer.

He works in a large room above a double garage some little distance from his house at Walton-on-Thames in Surrey. The room is fitted out like a luxurious executive suite, with its rows of bookshelves, filing cupboards, comfortable armchairs for visitors and a very substantial desk.

His method of working has never varied since early days. He begins a serial by painfully writing out every line in longhand, altering it considerably from time to time. When it appears to be in reasonable shape, he then types it on a portable machine. Next, he goes through it again carefully, marking further alterations, possibly adding a short scene or some extra lines of dialogue. Then he sends it to a typist, whose more professional version may have to be altered or completely re-typed, at least a dozen times if some improvements in the story have occurred to him in the interim.

He uses a tape recorder, but only to deal with correspondence and to register a sudden idea for a story which might otherwise be forgotten.

He usually gets his ideas whilst travelling. "A small incident might occur," he says. "A man picks up a wrong hat in a restaurant and for some unaccountable reasons this incident drops into my mind at a later date. I think about it, "stew it over" and eventually, very slowly, it sparks off a story idea. Don't ask me how, but it does."

At the start of a serial he carefully devises the complete story, working out in detail the necessary amount of action and suspense required for each episode.

Durbridge says that he finds the first episode the most difficult to write. "It's that blank piece of paper, staring up at you, challenging you to make a start."

He admits that the last episode is also a headache, for everything in the serial must be explained plausibly in this episode, which at the same time must contain the same quota of drama as the others.

When he has taken the complete set of neatly bound typescripts to the BBC he is immediately confronted with another set of problems. His television serials are preceded by the announcement: "Francis Durbridge Presents ..." which means that he has a share of the responsibility of seeing that the creatures of his imagination are being brought to life convincingly on the television screens. He must attend production conferences, auditions, rehearsal, and visit location spots.

At the end of it all he'll be as physically and mentally exhausted as an undergraduate who has just taken his Finals.

The Francis Durbridge stories are televised, broadcast and published in many languages and the author frequently visits the Continent to see the foreign versions of his serials. These days he also finds it necessary to travel extensively in search of ideas and documentary detail.

Generally speaking, however, he finds it difficult to write away from home. Only recently when Dino De Laurentiis, the Italian producer, asked him to live in Rome for some weeks at his company's expense while he wrote a film script, Durbridge insisted on doing the job at home.

His stories have a cosmopolitan aura – which is probably why they are popular in so many countries but he insists he creates them in familiar surroundings.

The Birmingham Post

www.ingramcontent.com/pod-product-compliance
Lightning Source LLC
Chambersburg PA
CBHW020835260626
47169CB00003B/998